SUSANNA SEES STARS

KU-216-087

ALSO BY MARY HOGAN

THE SERIOUS KISS

SUSANNA *sees* STARS

by

MARY HOGAN

SIMON AND SCHUSTER

SIMON AND SCHUSTER
First published in Great Britain in 2006
by Simon & Schuster UK Ltd
A CBS COMPANY

Copyright © 2006 by Mary Hogan
Cover image by www.blacksheep.co.uk

This book is copyright under the Berne Convention.
No reproduction without permission.
All rights reserved.

The right of Mary Hogan to be identified as the author of this work has been asserted by her in accordance with sections 77 and 78 of the Copyright, Designs and Patents Act, 1988.

1 3 5 7 9 10 8 6 4 2

Simon & Schuster UK Ltd
Africa House
64–78 Kingsway
London WC2B 6AH

A CIP catalogue record for this book is available from the British Library.

ISBN: 1 416 90157 4
EAN: 9781416901570

This book is a work of fiction. Names, characters, places and incidents are either products of the author's imagination or are used fictitiously. Any resemblance to actual events or locales or persons, living or dead, is entirely coincidental.

Set in 12/17 pt Adobe Garamond by
Rowland Phototypesetting Ltd, Bury St Edmunds, Suffolk
Printed and bound in Great Britain by Cox & Wyman, Reading, Berkshire

For Bob

ACKNOWLEDGEMENTS

Endless thanks to Ingrid Selberg for instantly making me feel at home, to Joanna Moult for her creativity and caring, to Venetia Gosling for pointing me in the right direction, to Elisa Offord for being as fun to hang out with as she is to work with, to Annette Green for her hard work on my behalf, and to Laura Langlie, for being supportive, talented, and tireless.

ONE

I am the luckiest girl in the world. What are the odds of *me,* celebrity junkie Susanna Barringer, native New Yorker, state school sophomore, more of a Roseanne than a Reese, landing a coveted summer gig at *Scene* magazine? It's got to be a gazillion to one. At *least.* But, here I am. Day One of the beginning of my life. My *real* life. Not the preamble of school and homework and obsessing over the zit on my chin that erupts each month like Mount Vesuvius.

'Aliens walk among us.' A bum in filthy brown clothes circles me as I wait for the cross-town bus. 'It could be me,' he says. 'It could be you.'

I flash him a thumbs-up and try not to breathe. His smell is so beyond BO there has to be a whole new name for it. Maybe some alien name like *Xoestryuuil* that only aliens understand. I mean, this guy reeks so bad he'd be jettisoned back to Earth if an alien abducted him. There aren't windows in a spaceship, are there? How could they *ever* air it out?

'The moon is in the seventh house. And Jupiter aligns with Mars,' he says.

Where have I heard that sentence before?

'Let peace guide the planet!' His Reekness yells to no one in particular. Frankly, his breath could use an Altoid, or a hundred. I consider tossing him my tin when I suddenly remember: that's a *song.* My parents sing it all the time. *And love will steer the stars.* It's from some ancient musical about hair. Even though my parents are too young to have been *true* hippies, they like to view themselves as former flower children. Which is laughable because Dad works in a forensics lab and Mom is the payroll manager for Bloomingdale's.

'Wake up, people! This is New York City! Crop circles are a crock! Aliens are *here,* on the streets. Look around!'

Glancing to my left, I see three upper east side divas with cheek implants and puffy, over-collagened lips and I think, well, *maybe.* Then I squint down the street and wonder when on Earth the bus is going to come.

It's eight-thirty on Monday morning and Manhattan is full of glum faces – and, of course, enough nut-jobs to make city life interesting. It's already so hot, my feet sink into the asphalt. My scalp is sweaty. The gutter smells like rotting oranges. Still, I can't stop smiling – even next to the guy who hasn't showered since the age of Aquarius. Unable to resist, I say it out loud: 'Intern at *Scene* magazine. You know, the *People* magazine clone?' I feel the words roll over my tongue. They taste incredibly sweet. I'll work directly for the editor-in-chief, Nell Wickham, who is considered a publishing genius.

I can picture it now: I'll have a pencil behind my ear, take notes in an editorial meeting, run off to get a scoop on Angelina, Jude, Paris or Johnny. A *teen* scoop. I'll ferret out the info kids want to know. Like, who told Lindsay Lohan she needed to lose weight? Or, do stars run to their dressing rooms to brush their teeth before a big love scene? If they don't, who has the worst breath in Hollywood?

Yeah, I know I'll be an assistant and have to do grunt work like all assistants do. Still, I wonder, how soon will they issue me my own business cards?

'Their eyes,' Mr Stinkbomb warns me on the street. 'That's how you can tell they are aliens. Huge pupils.'

I lower my lids and look the other way. You can never be too careful in New York. I have no idea if my pupils are large or small.

Finally, the bus arrives and I escape the stink and the steam, stepping into a deliciously cool blast of air-conditioning. As I make my way to an open seat, I inhale some woman's perfume and think: Ah! The sweet smell of success!

Nobody can believe I scored such an awesome summer job. Not my parents, nor my best friend, Amelia. The only other job I've ever had was babysitting my brothers and walking my neighbour's dog once when she broke her leg.

The way it all came about was pure destiny.

I couldn't sleep. It was the middle of the night, in my

freshman year. I was at that 'questioning phase' every kid hits eventually. I was like, when will I *ever* use algebra? Why am I killing myself to learn all this useless information? My dad is a *scientist* and even he doesn't use algebra. I was searching for the deeper meaning of homework and coming up empty.

I was desperate for answers. So I turned on the TV.

'You have the power to do exactly what you want with your life.'

A guy with a humungous head spoke to me from a cable infomercial. He had a microphone strapped to his ear. His teeth were so white, they lit up my dark bedroom.

'It's a matter of listening to your *soul* and letting the universe guide you,' he said.

'Yeah,' I said out loud. 'What universe cares about algebra?'

I got real quiet and listened to my soul.

At first, it was hard hearing my soul with the TV on. Plus, my biology teacher's voice kept intruding in my head, telling me to memorise the difference between meiosis and mitosis so I could ace tomorrow's quiz. (Another waste of time! Like my cells will stop dividing if I flunk my test!) But when I muted both sounds, something awesome happened. I swear I heard a squeaky voice – oddly high-pitched for an entire *universe* – tell me I was destined to dish celebrity dirt. No lie! I know it's shallow for someone's *destiny* to be a gossip, but who says the universe is always deep? Who am I to question cosmic orders?

The down-and-dirty truth is, I've always been overly-fascinated with showbiz. I say 'overly' because I *do* recognise that most kids with my Grade Point Average (three point six and rising) know more about cell division than, say, the fact that Cameron Diaz spends an obscene amount of air minutes talking with her buddies on her cell phone. I realise that my best friend Amelia thinks I'm crazy because I have a recurring dream that I live in *Smallville* with Tom Welling. When I wake up – in that delicious moment between 'asleep' and 'awake' – I swear I can hear Superman snoring next to me.

My parents are horrified. Dad's idea of light reading is *Scientific American*.

'You realise you may be compromising the nerve fibres in your corpus callosum,' he said one time when he saw me watching *Entertainment Tonight*.

'Huh?'

'My point exactly!'

Mom once asked me, 'How could anyone still care why Gwyneth named her daughter Apple?' after seeing a headline in the check-out line at D'Agostino's.

'For the same reason we're still agog that Jermaine Jackson named his son Jermajesty, Demi named her daughter Rumer, and Toni Braxton thinks her son is a pair of jeans by naming him Denim,' I said, indignant.

I still remember the appalled expression on my mom's face. It's the same look she gave me when she found an issue of *Star* magazine hidden under my mattress. Most parents would be that upset if they found a bag of weed.

If I channel Dr Phil, I'd have to say that's one reason why I'm addicted to celebrity dirt. Forbidden fruit, you know? My parents never allowed me to watch network TV when I was a kid, or read anything that wasn't 'mind-expanding'. (I didn't have my own TV until I was in middle school!)

Another reason is probably deeper – more Freudian than afternoon *insta-shrink.* I was an only child for a very long time. My three brothers – Evan, Henry and Sam – were born when I was fourteen. (Can you believe my parents dethroned me with *triplets*?!) Before The Trips were born, when I wasn't hanging out with my best friend, Mel, I spent a lot of time alone. Celebs were probably my version of imaginary friends. Friends who looked perfect and had problems that were solved in twenty-two minutes or less. Friends I probably wanted to be, seeing as how I was chubby and curly-haired and felt as though I'd never feel even slightly normal.

My baby brothers are *soooo* cute and I love them *soooo* much. But, let's get real. When you're navigating adolescence, one baby around the apartment is hard enough. Three? Well, you've never seen so many bodily secretions in your life. It's all my parents can do to keep the baby-wipes in motion. They stopped having time for me the moment my brothers' diapers stopped being soiled with baby poo and started loading up with *poop.*

Now, at the mature age of fifteen, I'm working on cultivating inner peace. In spite of the fact that I live in a madhouse. I'm striving to wipe my brothers' snot with a

Zen-like reverence for nature. I'm learning to *embrace* my flaws. Each morning, I tell my thighs that it's okay to touch at the top. I greet frizzy-hair days with a hardy, 'Hey there!' And that 'being normal' thing, well, it doesn't take a forensic scientist to tell me it's not in my DNA. Might as well let it go.

None of this works very well. But, I'm quite sure Dr Phil would say it's worth the effort to keep trying. Especially now that I'm a role model for my brothers. Only, he'd say it in some down-home way that would make everyone chuckle.

When I awoke the morning after my soul-listening, I had the *Frankenguru's* advice in my brain. Right after my biology quiz (I got a B plus, instead of an A, because I forgot to include the step when the reproductive cells, gametes, are produced!), I decided to embrace my superficiality too, and follow my universal bliss. I composed a letter, typed it into the school library computer, printed it out, and sent a copy to every celebrity magazine in New York.

'Dear blah, blah . . . my name is Susanna Barringer, blah, blah . . . I'd like to be a summer intern at your magazine, blah, blah, blah . . .'

Then, I waited. I was so sure the universe would take care of everything, I actually carried my cell with me into the bathroom so I wouldn't miss the call. After a week passed, I obsessively checked my email. After two weeks, I raced for the mail each day after school. After a month of stone-cold silence, I stopped watching stupid infomercials by guys who can't fit their fat head into a hat.

That's roughly the time I starred in my own reality show and realised I might be dreaming the impossible dream. The trip from my neighbourhood in the meat-packing district to the Midtown offices of New York Publishing was a bus or subway ride, but light years from possibility. What made me think I could snag an internship when I'm still in high school? At a national magazine, no less! Had my soul really been telling me to *shovel* dirt instead of *dish* it?

Clearly, I had a few (thousand!) obstacles in my path. Which, honestly, only firmed up my resolve. Hey, I'm a native New Yorker. Giving up isn't in my pedigree. Negative odds are so *negative,* you know? Why let them bring you down? The way I figured it, my only chance at success was to stand out, be different, dare to think outside the box. Which, oddly enough, spawned the idea that got me the gig at *Scene* magazine.

Like I said, it was pure *destiny.*

TWO

Summer vacation was only three weeks away. My letters were all a washout. The rich kids in my school were planning to bake on the beaches near their family vacation homes in the Hamptons or at the New Jersey shore. The rest of us – me, included – were trying to avoid baking on the streets of New York. Or worse, getting a daily grease facial over the fry pit at McDonald's.

If my latest idea – fifty per cent inspiration, fifty per cent desperation – didn't work, I would be toast.

Here's what I did: after school one afternoon, I took the downtown bus to Chinatown. Snaking through the tourist mobs on Canal Street, I found a little shop that sold little stuff, and I bought a tiny lockbox complete with mini lock and key. Then, I hopped back on the bus and returned home. Inspired by my fabulous find, I printed out a note to the head of my favourite magazine – Nell Wickham, *Scene*'s editor-in-chief. Folding the note into a small square, I tucked it neatly inside the box. The first line read: *I hear magazine jobs are tough to break into.*

Amelia informed me that the grammar was all wrong.

'You can't end a sentence with a preposition,' she said.

I *knew* that. But, what am I going to write? *I hear magazine jobs are tough into which to break?*

I don't think so.

So, I went with my gut. I left the bad grammar in and included a funny section about how I'd been born with a silver tape recorder in my mouth, how I was destined to interview celebrities. I confessed to dreaming of standing on red carpets shouting, 'Who are you wearing?!' I speculated that Joan Rivers was probably my *real* mom, and Melissa and I were switched at birth. Then I locked the letter inside the box. Using my babysitting money, I Fed Ex'd the lockbox to *Scene* magazine. The next day, I messengered the key.

You have the power to unlock my potential, I wrote, on a long, white ribbon I tied to the key. *If you give me a summer job, Ms Wickham, I'll give you a girl who will do anything to get a great story.*

Amelia thought the 'anything' line was too much. 'Would you hide in a celebrity's garbage can?' she asked.

'Maybe,' I said.

She added, 'If there was dog poop in it?'

I rolled my eyes and told her she was missing the point. 'It's about getting attention,' I said. 'Nell Wickham isn't going to hire me if I just ask her nicely.'

Less than a week after I sent the lockbox and key, Nell Wickham's executive assistant completely blew me away by calling to set up an interview. I couldn't wait to hang up the phone so I could whoop like a maniac. I mean, what are the odds? Incredibly, I was on my way. Thank you, universe! Late-night cable! Move over, Joan and Melissa.

Mom let me use her employee discount to buy an interview outfit at Bloomingdale's. It took all day Saturday to select the perfect look: a cotton floral shift and lime-green Kate Spadeish handbag. I completed the outfit with my favourite pink patent-leather knock-off JP Tod loafers. I even rubbed fake-tanning cream on my white legs.

Monday moved as slowly as ketchup that you just *know* is never going to pour out. I could hear the seconds clicking off in my head all day at school. My interview was scheduled for four o'clock. To keep my outfit fresh, I brought it to school in a garment bag. No way would I have enough time to race home and change. Not when I had to make it to Midtown in forty-five minutes. So, I carried everything with me all day. The moment the final bell rang, I dashed into the bathroom and peeled off my sweaty clothes. Amelia guarded the door.

'Did you remember deodorant?' she asked.

'Yes.'

'Toothpaste?'

'Yes.'

'Talc?'

'Talc?'

'You know, to soak up sweat in nooks and crannies.'

I rolled my eyes. 'Could you please zip me up?'

While Mel zipped the back of my dress, I brushed my teeth, splashed cold water on my face, blotted with a paper towel, and applied a thin layer of the tinted moisturiser I bought at Duane Reade drug store. I swiped my lips in gloss, my cheeks in blush, my lids in shadow, my lashes in mascara. I brushed my hair and twisted it in a messy knot, held firm with a pink claw clip. Completing the look, I slid my bare feet into my loafers and dangled my new green handbag on my forearm.

'Fabulous!' I said to my reflection in the bathroom mirror.

Mel hugged me and said, 'You look like a spring garden!'

By the time I rose up from the subway in Midtown, I looked like a wilted spring salad. I wished I *had* sprinkled talc on all my nooks and crannies. While the individual subway cars are air-conditioned (most of the time), the platform is always a sauna. And the street is one big steam room. Still, it was thrilling to be walking into my destiny. Even though I could feel my bare feet squishing around inside my fake-leather loafers.

Midtown Manhattan is Publishing Central. You can almost smell freshly-printed pages on the streets. Everyone walks fast with a cell pressed to their ears. They emit an aura of mega-money deals. Unless they're wearing the 'New York Tourist' uniform: oversized T-shirt tucked into undersized high-waisted shorts; thick leather sandals with socks. In that case, you have to power-walk around them. Which is just what I did when I saw the polished brass revolving doors ahead, leading into the lobby of *Scene* magazine.

'I have an appointment with Nell Wickham,' I said to the guard, blowing sweaty fringe off my forehead.

The ground-floor lobby of *Scene* magazine was panelled in rich, dark wood. The floor was forest-green granite. Mercifully, it was super air-conditioned.

'ID, please,' the uniformed guard said.

After I produced my school identification, he called someone, said my name, then hung up.

'Seventeenth floor,' he said.

My heart fluttered. I was truly on my way up.

THREE

Seventeen floors, I discovered the day my destiny began, is the perfect amount of time to dry sweat. By the time the elevator doors opened with a gentle *whoosh*, I was feeling revived. I was also feeling a frazzled mix of thrill and terror. My knees wobbled as I stepped into the reception area.

The first thing I saw were the gleaming gold letters on the shiny mahogany wall spelling the word, *Scene.* I nearly burst into tears. My emotions were that overloaded. It was like a doctor's office. Silent. The brown leather couch was empty. The only person in the whole area was a stunning receptionist sitting behind a dark wood desk. A Britney-esque microphone curled around her cheek. She lifted her perfectly-plucked eyebrows in my direction as if to say, 'Come closer. Let me help you.'

'I'm Susanna Barringer,' I said, trying to steady my voice.

She looked me up and down, sneered, and said, 'So?'

My smile drooped. 'I have an appointment with Nell Wickham. An interview,' I added to let her know I wasn't just *anybody.*

Looking bored, the receptionist pressed a button on the phone with the eraser of her pencil.

'Nell's interview is here,' she said into her mike.

The receptionist then pressed another button on the phone and a button on her desk. I heard a buzz.

'Carmen will meet you,' she said.

Following the buzz, trying to calm my thudding heart, I made my way to the door that lead into *Scene*'s inner sanctum.

'Thank yo—'

The beautiful receptionist had already turned away. I didn't care. I was entering Oz.

The difference between *Scene* magazine's silent reception area and the editorial bullpen was the difference between being disinvited to the coolest party in the world and personally knowing the band. I felt like I'd walked into the middle of the dance floor. Super-skinny women dressed in black scurried back and forth. Guys with shaggy hair and just-right stubble shouted thrilling words like 'masthead', 'page-proofs', and 'four-colour spreads'. Clicking computer keys sounded like a thousand tiny tap-dancers. Land-line phones were cradled on shoulders, cells chirped with a hundred different rings. Everyone was loud.

'What's that? You're breaking up.'

'Thalia, get me the Lopez file!'

'Who made this tea? It's vile.'

'When Ashton's people call, put them straight through.'

It was a huge room full of desks and grey tweed partitions. In-boxes overflowed with paper. The air smelled like hair gel. It was as exhilarating as it was terrifying.

'Susanna?'

A woman about as old as my mom walked up to me. She had black hair in a neat ponytail, and wore red lipstick. Her body was normal-sized, and her dress was the colour of mocha ice-cream.

'I'm Carmen,' she said, warmly. 'Nell's executive assistant.'

Carmen held out her hand. I shook it. She said, 'I'm sure you feel like you've landed on Mars. This place can be a bit intimidating at first. But don't worry, you're going to be fine.'

She read my mind. I loved her instantly.

'Pay no attention to Astrid,' Carmen said. 'She growls because she's hungry. Have you seen how tiny her waist is?'

My full smile returned. Though my heart was still pounding, Carmen relaxed me. As I followed her through the beehive of an office, I felt my shoulders drop, my heart rate slow and the fresh swipe of deodorant in my armpits stop working overtime.

'Nell?' Carmen poked her head in a large office at the far corner of the room. 'Susanna Barringer is here for the special internship.'

Special? I beamed.

A deep voice with a British accent said, 'Send her in.'

Carmen made a Vanna White gesture with her arm and

mouthed the words 'good luck'. I swept into Nell Wickham's office with my head held high.

'Sit,' Nell said, not looking up from whatever she was reading.

I sat.

Everything in Nell Wickham's office was either bright white or gleaming glass – even Nell herself, who was dressed in a milk-white suit. The couch, cushioned chairs, drapes, carpeting, were all the colour of first snow. Definitely not the room where you want to start your period, I thought.

Nell was *gorgeous.* She had soft blonde hair that gently brushed her shoulders, smooth white skin, a small pointed nose and the most beautiful clothes I'd ever seen. Plus, her accent made her sound so classy. Like the way she said 'sit'. If an American had said it, I would have felt like a dog.

'Your lockbox idea was very clever,' she said, looking up.

'Well, I—'

'I like clever.'

Grinning, I said, 'I try my bes—'

'But not too clever. Do you know what I mean?'

I had no clue.

'Yes, of course,' I lied. 'Too clever is the worst.'

'Where else have you worked?' she asked me, suddenly.

I gulped.

'Nowhere *per se*,' I said, deciding that a babysitting and dog-walking resumé might hurt my impending career more than help it.

'Per se?'

'I'm in high school.'

'Oh.'

Oops. Had I forgotten to mention that little tidbit? Nell looked like she'd sucked a lemon. I hadn't lied, but I hadn't exactly highlighted it, either. I suppose my quip about being switched at birth with Melissa Rivers might have led her astray. After all, Melissa is a *mom.*

'I'm available all summer,' I added, semi-cleverly.

'I see,' she said. Then she sighed. A big long one. Followed by a silence so lengthy I thought I might have spontaneously gone deaf. My nooks and crannies got damp. I felt myself shrinking. Clearly, the cotton floral shift that had looked *so* chic in Bloomie's was all wrong for *Scene* magazine. I looked like an Olsen twin before she grew up and became hot. *Way* before she stopped eating. And a pink claw clip? What was I thinking?

'You may be perfect,' Nell said, at last.

Perfect? My face lit up.

'We're considering launching a teen version of *Scene* magazine in the future and I'd like to hire someone who can be my window into young adults,' Nell said.

'That's me,' I blurted. 'A window. I'm completely see-through.'

Nell cocked one eyebrow and scanned me up and down.

'I'm looking for someone *ordinary*,' she said. 'No ivy-leaguers.'

'I go to state school!' I nearly sang. 'Yale would laugh if I applied. Harvard would fall over. I'm not even a good athlete!'

Nell recrossed her long legs under the glass desk and said, 'It's so easy to lose touch with – well, *average* people when you're – well, *me.*'

Thank God I wore a cotton floral! I slid my feet out from under my chair so she could see my knock-off Tods. I was suddenly grateful that my faux tan looked a tad streaky.

'You'd work directly for me, Susan,' Nell said.

'It's *Susanna.*' Then, trying to give her a peek through the window of an average, ordinary teen, I added, 'Working for you would be cool.'

'It's only a summer internship,' Nell said.

'Awesome.'

'Can you start tomorrow?'

'Uh, school doesn't let out for two weeks,' I said, swallowing hard.

'Fine. See you in two weeks.'

'Really?'

Nell nodded, then resumed reading whatever was on her desk. Her feet were visible beneath her glass desk. The toes of her white shoes could pop a balloon.

'Thank you, Ms Wickham,' I sputtered, stunned.

'Good God, Susan, call me Nell.'

FOUR

Here I am. Day One of my destiny.

For the past two weeks, I've obsessed over what to wear. Black, so I fit in with the staff at *Scene*? White, so I match my boss? Or the ordinary clothes of an ordinary teen, so Nell will get her peek into reality? Ultimately, I decided to wear what I already owned, since I discovered that internships don't pay a cent, and Mom cut me off from her Bloomingdale's discount because, she said, 'It's ridiculous to expect a kid to dress like an adult.'

Feeling the *Scene* magazine elevator carry me upward, I smooth the khaki skirt and orange rayon T-shirt I bought a few months ago at Old Navy. What's more 'average teen' than Old Navy?

'Good morning, Astrid,' I say, as I step onto the seventeenth floor and approach the reception desk.

'It's *Ah*-strid,' she snaps.

'Ah. Got it.' I place a paper bag on her desk. 'I brought you a blueberry muffin.'

She opens the bag, peers in. 'Five hundred and seventy.'

'No, a dollar fifty. I bought it downstairs.'

'Calories!' *Ah*-strid looks like she might breathe fire. 'Get it off my desk.'

Quickly, I remove the bag.

'Sorry,' I stammer.

Astrid raises one eyebrow and lowers her voice. 'Let's get something straight,' she says. 'You are an *intern.* I don't talk to interns. I don't socialise with them, and I certainly don't eat disgusting store-bought muffins they dump on my desk with their grubby intern hands. Got it?'

I blink. 'Got it,' I say.

Astrid buzzes me in. Clutching the muffin bag, I push through the office door. I feel stunned. It's as if she took the muffin and schmushed in it my face. But, the moment I enter the office, I shake it off. Why let anyone get me down when it's Day One of my destiny? I'm a budding teen reporter! I've landed the internship of a lifetime! What could possibly ruin the most awesome opportunity ever?

'Susanna!' Carmen greets me with a huge hug. 'Welcome to *Scene* magazine.'

Inhaling the aroma of coffee and fresh nail polish, I smile and say to myself, 'I am the luckiest girl in the world.' From now on, I'll call *Ah*-strid *Ass*-trid behind her back. So there.

Scurrying along beside Carmen, I struggle to keep up as she takes me on a speed-tour of the office.

'The fashion department is here, the celebrity library is over there, the art department is down that hall.'

Carmen points and waves and occasionally stops one of the beautiful people who fly past us.

'This is Renée, the senior editor.' Renée has light-red hair and dark-black glasses. She looks as hungry as *Ass*-trid.

'Nice to meet yo—'

'Hi. Bye. Sorry.' Renée shakes my hand, then dashes off.

'We're closing,' Carmen explains. 'It's not usually this crazed.'

'Closing?'

'Putting the issue to bed. Things chill out next week when the cycle begins again. Sasha!'

A gorgeous woman, at least six-feet tall, with the smoothest brown skin I've ever seen, slams on her brakes and whirls around.

'This is Susanna, Nell's new intern,' Carmen says. To me, she adds, 'Sasha is the fashion editor.'

'Nice to meet yo—'

'You're young,' Sasha says, narrowing her eyes at me.

'I'm fifteen,' I mumble, feeling like I'm five.

'Fifteen?!'

'Nell wants a kid around for the summer,' Carmen explains.

Starting with my hair, and ending with my brown leather sandals, Sasha absorbs my whole being before saying, 'You need help.'

'Help?'

'Lose the prehistoric shoes. After closing, meet me in the closet and I'll hook you up.'

'Huh?'

Sasha races off and Carmen continues the tour. 'The restrooms are over there, coffee and vending machines are in the break room, the photo department is over there, and . . .'

Carmen keeps talking and pointing, but suddenly, all I can hear is the pulsing of blood in my ears. My eyes lock on a guy looking at a colour photo of Paris Hilton.

He wears a purple bandana tied low on his forehead, and a bright-white wife-beater T-shirt. At *work.* Only, it looks perfect. Very *GQ.* His jeans are low enough to see where his tan line stops, which sounds kind of cheesy, but this guy doesn't look cheesy in anything. He's the kind of guy who's always been so good-looking, it's no big deal. He just throws clothes on and they adjust themselves perfectly to his awesome bod.

'Who's that?' I ask.

Carmen grins. 'That is Keith Franklin. Our senior photographer. Keith!'

Keith Franklin looks up from Paris Hilton and gazes at me. His eyes are impossibly blue – the colour of the Mediterranean in a commercial about sailing the Greek isles. As he calmly walks toward me, my cheeks instantly flush red. My nooks and crannies get soggy again.

'This is Susanna, Keith. Nell's new intern.'

Keith leans in and kisses my burning cheek. He smells like a Graham cracker. I feel faint.

'What will you be doing?' he asks.

I open my mouth, but nothing comes out. Carmen answers for me.

'Whatever Nell wants.'

Keith laughs. 'Just like the rest of us.' Turning around, he casually makes his way back to Paris.

As I examine Keith Franklin from behind, my heart skips in my chest. Is this what guys look like in the working world? How does anything ever get done? Slowly, I regain feeling in my legs.

'The administrative offices are on the sixteenth floor.' Carmen continues the tour. I calm my pulse and hurry to keep up. 'But our world is right here in this room. Senior editors have corner offices, associate editors have cubicles along the windows, reporters are out in the field, assistant editors have cubbies in the middle of the room, fact-checkers and editorial assistants have desks along the wall, and your table is *here.*'

She stops in front of a storage closet. My table sits in a small alcove just to the left of it, not far from the Xerox machine and paper shredder. The only thing on it is a phone and a computer.

'At least you don't have to go far to get office supplies,' Carmen says, laughing. I laugh, too. I know I'm just an intern and don't even rate a *desk.* I know I have to prove myself. But, what no one at *Scene* magazine knows yet, is that I am Susanna Barringer, native New Yorker, clever and ambitious and willing to do whatever I have to do (even sift through poopy garbage!) to get a great story and show Nell that I'll make a great celebrity-reporter. I recognise that I've been given an incredible opportunity and I'm not going to waste it. This is going to be the most exciting summer of my life.

'Get yourself settled in,' Carmen says. 'All you need to know is, when Nell calls, come running.'

FIVE

'Susan!'

Who knew Nell would call me by using her lungs instead of the phone?

'Are you out there? *Susan!*'

I arrive at Nell's office door, pad in hand, pencil behind my ear, ready to embark on my first assignment as a teen intern. I'm settled in and ready to let Nell Wickham peer through the window of my teenage soul. Inspiration? Thy name is *Susanna.*

'I'm feeling peckish,' Nell says.

'Peckish?'

'Starbucks has a fabulous sugar-free pecan brownie. Only three net carbs. And a latte. Iced. Skimmed.'

I stand there, mulling over the word, 'peckish'.

'Go!'

Startled, I wheel around.

'Susan!'

I wheel back around.

'Splenda,' Nell says.

'You're welcome,' I reply.

Nell rolls her eyes. 'Don't forget the Splenda sweetener, Susan. I can't stand Equal and real sugar will launch me on a bread binge.'

Oh.

'Anything else?' I ask.

'Well,' Nell sighs dramatically, 'now that you mention it, shut the door.'

'Shut the door?'

'Come here,' Nell whispers.

I shut the door, take a step toward my new boss.

'Closer,' Nell says.

I shuffle nearer, not at all comfortable with this turn of events.

'*Closer.*'

My heart is pounding. Gripping the edge of her glass desk, I lean in so far I'm nearly touching Nell's nose.

'Be honest,' she says, 'can you see my pores?'

Can I see her pores? This close, her face is a slab of Swiss cheese. I can see the hairs up her nostrils!

'Pores?' I repeat, stalling. Clearly, there is a right answer, and one that can get me fired from the first day of my non-paying destiny. I say, 'Not from here, no.'

Nell beams and claps her hands.

'The micro-dermabrasion facials are working! Brilliant!'

The Starbucks on Fifth Avenue is a block and a half away. Just enough time for me to start sweating again.

There's a short line inside, but I go directly to the pastry case. As I scan right and left – crumb cake, black and white cookies, Rice Krispies bars – I feel panic surging in my veins. No low-carb brownies! Would she accept a lemon bar instead? A biscotti?

'Nell Wickham's new intern?' the counter girl asks me.

My head jerks up. 'How did you know?'

'I've seen that deer-in-the-headlights look before. You'll be in here a lot,' she says. 'I'm Willow.'

Willow's black hair is streaked with magenta. Her eyebrow stud is silver. The brim of her Starbucks hat is turned up and worn sideways.

'I'm Susanna,' I say. 'It's my first day.'

Willow nods knowingly. 'Don't worry, Susanna. We keep a private stash of brownies in the back for Nell. She has an account.'

'Thank God,' I whisper under my breath. I was worried I would have to pay for Nell's stuff myself. She didn't give me any money, and I was too nervous to ask.

'I'll need an iced skim latte, too,' I say. 'Or, did you already know that?'

Willow nods in a superior way. Then she disappears for a moment to get Nell's brownie. When she returns, she starts on the iced latte and asks, 'Want a piece of advice?'

'Yes. How *do* you get the foam so fluffy?'

'They have a queen.'

My nose wrinkles in confusion. 'Starbucks?'

'The Brits,' Willow says, 'they have a *queen.* They have royalty and castles and Cinderella coaches.'

'What are you talking about?' I glance at my watch. Will Nell be timing my first Starbucks run?

'Nell Wickham grew up in a country that firmly separates royalty from commoners. It's not like America, where everyone believes they can become President. In Nell's mind, you're a commoner and she's a queen. Period. That's the way it is. She'll have no problem treating you like a servant. She probably *had* servants when she was a kid. She won't feel the slightest inclination to help you achieve anything. You'll have to do it all on your own.'

My mouth hangs open. 'How do you know this?' I ask.

'I did a paper on her.'

'For school?'

'NYU,' she says, 'Sociology class. I got an A.'

She beams. 'All I'm saying is, don't take it personally. That's my advice. Nell lives in a kingdom all her own.'

Nodding, I take the brownie and iced skim latte and run back to *Scene,* hoping that Queen Nell won't notice how long I was gone.

SIX

There's a huge commotion in the reception area when I return. Young, black-clad editors are milling around. I look for Keith Franklin's purple bandana, but don't see him. I don't see any of the other senior editors I met, either. The air is buzzing. Even *Ass*-trid is animated.

'He's tall,' she says. 'Usually, actors are so short.'

'Who?' I ask. 'Who's tall?'

Ass-trid ignores me. A pre-anorexic, post-teen, blonde-haired assistant named Francesca says, 'When he smiled at me, I nearly fainted.'

'Who?' I ask. 'Who smiled?'

Francesca ignores me. One of the other editorial assistants asks, 'Is he giving Nell an exclusive? Is that why he's here?'

'Who?' I ask. 'Who's here?'

'Brad Pitt!' Francesca finally snaps at me. 'God, you sound like an owl.'

Brad Pitt is *here*? In Nell's office? My heart races. I dash for the door, but *Ass*-trid refuses to buzz me in. Even when I pound on the door, she won't press the release button.

'Senior staff only,' she says, sneering.

'Celebrity lock-out,' one of the assistants explains. 'Whenever a big star drops by, they herd us nobodies into the reception area so we won't gawk.'

Brad Pitt is only yards away and I can't gawk. I groan.

'There has to be another way in,' I say.

'There's not,' Francesca answers impatiently. 'We tried when Nicole Kidman was here. You have to wait until they leave. You can gawk – subtly – while they wait for the elevator.'

Francesca turns to one of the other assistants and says, 'Remember Nicole's skin? If I had skin like that, I'd never have wasted it on Tom Cruise.'

They titter, but I don't have time to eavesdrop. Brad Pitt soon to be in our elevator? I think fast. There are three elevator cars. That's a thirty-three-and-a-third per cent chance that he'll ride the one I'm on. (Maybe Math *isn't* a waste of time!) I stash Nell's iced latte and low-carb brownie in the reception waiting room, press the 'down' button and wait for the elevator to arrive.

'It's his jaw line,' someone says. 'Same with Johnny Depp. Their jaws are works of art.'

Frantically, I press the 'down' button a few more times. Finally, one elevator door opens on the seventeenth floor and I hop on. Two other people are in the car. The three of us ride down in silence. In the lobby, the doors open and my co-passengers get off. Not me. I press 'seventeen' and ride right back up.

For the next hour and fifteen minutes, I ride up and down. People get on and off. I stand at the buttons and ask, 'Floor?'

'After you,' a man in a grey suit says in the lobby, holding the elevator doors open.

'No, thanks,' I say. 'I'm going back up.'

And I do. I smile at people who get on. I memorise the wood panelling. I even wave at the security camera. By now, they must wonder who I am.

After about forty minutes, I start to feel nauseous. But, I don't care. I have a thirty-three-and-a-third percent chance of riding seventeen floors with Brad Pitt. What's a little motion sickness when the odds are one in *three*?

As I rise and fall, I compose questions in my head.

'Did you hear the whole world moan when you broke up with Jen?'

No, I say to myself, he'll clamp that gorgeous jaw shut at the mention of Jen, Angelina, or any other probe into his personal life.

'When you were crowned "Sexiest Man Alive", how did it feel to be dethroned by Pierce Brosnan?'

No way, Susanna! Brad will roll his eyes at that one. Come up with something fresh.

'What's the first thing you bought with your first big paycheck?'

I groan. That was so long ago, he'll never remember.

Up and down, up and down, I rack my brain. Appeal to his playful, impish side, Susanna. Catch him off-guard.

Ask him something no one has ever asked him before.

Suddenly, I've got it! When Brad Pitt steps on the elevator, I'll *ignore* him. I'll adopt an *Ass*-trid face and look bored. Maybe, I'll even sigh. Yes! I'll sigh. I'll say, 'Floor?'

He'll say, 'Lobby.'

I'll press 'one'. We'll both stare at the numbers as they light up. Sixteen, fifteen, fourteen. I'll sigh again just to calm my heart. Six, five, four.

Just before the elevator doors open on the first floor, I'll whip around and ask Brad Pitt, 'If your prom date called you today, would you talk to her?'

He'll laugh. He'll be so stunned, he'll answer honestly. And I, Susanna Barringer, will have a *scoop*.

Brilliant!

When my watch tells me I've been riding the elevator for an hour and *sixteen* minutes, the doors open on the seventeenth floor and the reception area is empty. I hop off.

'Where is everybody?' I ask *Ass*-trid.

'At work,' she says.

'But, Brad—'

'Gone.'

'Gone?'

'I only say things once,' she says, once.

'But, I had a thirty-three-and-a-third per cent chance,' I say, whimpering. Brad took another elevator?

Without another word, *Ass*-trid points to Nell's Starbucks stash and buzzes me into the editorial bullpen. The latte is watery and the brownie is gooey. Queen Nell will not be pleased. But all I care about at the moment is the fact that the celebrity lock-out is over and I'm scoopless.

SEVEN

'Sue!'

It's Day Two. I'm wearing another Old Navy skirt (denim) and a white cotton blouse from the Gap. I 'lost' the brown sandals as Sasha suggested and am wearing my pink knock-off Tods.

'Sue!'

I'm tempted to inform Nell that it takes a few seconds to unbend my legs, get up from my table and run into her office. She needn't scream for me. I'm also tempted to suggest she call me by my actual name. But, Willow's words are running through my head. Queen Nell lives in her own kingdom.

'Make a copy of this, then deliver the original as soon as possible,' she says, handing me a manuscript. 'The writer won't leave his air-conditioned apartment in the summer, and I need a rewrite by Friday.'

'Okay,' I say, and turn to leave.

'On your way back, pick up the baby gift I ordered at Petit Bâteau.'

'Where is that?'

She stares. 'How should I know?'

I nod. Turn to leave.

'Tea.'

'Excuse me?'

'Iced green tea would be lovely. Not Chai. Regular green tea. Brew it yourself. Yes. Make it fresh.'

'Now?'

'Of course *now.* Why wouldn't I want it now?'

Hesitating, I wait for the next command.

'Now means *now*, Sue.'

'It's Susanna, actually,' I say.

Nell stares at me blankly. I turn and scurry out.

'One more thing,' she shouts after me.

I scurry back.

'I'm off carbs. Find me something *proteinish* to have for lunch.'

'Like . . . *meat*?' I ask.

'Don't they teach you about protein in that state school you attend?'

She curls her lips and says 'state school' like it's an outhouse.

'What are you waiting for?' Nell asks.

This time, I turn and *run* so she doesn't have the chance to call me back – by *any* name.

In the break room, while waiting for the tea water to boil,

Francesca marches up to me. She wears a narrow black skirt and cap-sleeved black shirt.

'You're Susanna, right?'

'Right,' I say. 'Not Susan, Anna, Sue, or Suzanne.'

Francesca stares as blankly as Nell had.

'I'm Renée's assistant,' she says. 'Francesca.'

'We met in the recep—'

'Yeah,' she says, cutting me off. 'Renée asked me to give you this list.'

'List?'

'She needs a few things picked up before tomorrow's shoot.'

'Oh,' I say. 'I'm on my way to run a gazillion errands for Nell.'

Ignoring me, Francesca shoves the list in my hand. The first item reads: *tampons*.

'Renée needs tampons for a photo shoot?' I ask.

'That's for me,' she says. 'You don't mind, do you? Of course not. I'd do it for you. I'm swamped today. Thanks, uh – what's your name again? Sue? Oh, never mind. I'll just forget it.'

Francesca twirls on her pointy heels and leaves. If the whistle on the tea kettle weren't screaming, I'd still be standing in the break room with my mouth hanging open.

I know it's only been two days, but the image of my brilliant teen internship is already fading under the harsh light of reality. Nell appears to have no intention of gazing through the window of my teenhood. In fact, the only time she talks to me at all is to get something for her or tell her how she looks. When I came in this morning, she asked, 'Do I look puffy to you?'

'Puffy?'

'Bloated. Water-retentive.'

I looked at her. Suddenly, I noticed that her lips *did* look puffy. They were positively swollen. Like the time my brother, Evan, ate shrimp. His lips blossomed before our eyes. We thought he'd soon rise up to the ceiling.

'Yes,' I said. 'Your lips are definitely puffed out. Did you eat shrimp?'

Nell scoffed. 'I was injected this morning.'

'With shrimp?'

'Collagen, you dolt.'

I had no idea what a dolt was, but I could tell by her tone it wasn't flattering.

'I'm talking about my *body*,' Nell said, annoyed. 'Does it look engorged with water?'

Again, I examined my boss. This time, I looked to see if she looked anything like I always do ten days before my period.

'No. Absolutely not. No signs of bloating. You look normal.'

'Brilliant!' she said, beaming. 'I was naughty last night and had salt on the rim of my margarita. I was up until dawn trying to pee it out, but I couldn't. This morning, my toes looked like tiny Vienna sausages. See?'

She thrust bare feet out from under her desk. Like everything else on her body, they looked perfect to me.

'Ah,' I said.

'Today, I'm going to drink nothing but water to flush the salt out. Bring me a litre of Aquafina, will you Susie?'

Susie? I nodded and turned to leave, when Nell said, 'And a scone. Wholegrain cinnamon. I'm feeling a tad peckish.'

Before I left my boss's office, I checked her pupils to see if she was an alien. Frankly, they *did* look frightfully big.

But, here in the break room, Nell's not-Chai tea is ready, the agoraphobic writer is waiting for me and Francesca may be bleeding into her thong. No time to ponder my predicament – the steamy, stinky city streets await.

EIGHT

When all is said and done, is anything better than sleep?

'Susanna?'

My bed is the most luscious spot on Earth. Perhaps in the entire galaxy. The mattress is state-of-the-art – not really a mattress as much as a *resting system.* It naturally conforms to my body and swallows me up when I lie down. Mom bought it for me last year when she read an article in the *New York Times* about sleep deprivation and kids. She figured I'd get straight As if I got eight solid hours a night.

'I *am* tired all the time,' I told her, not mentioning that I'm addicted to *The Daily Show with Jon Stewart.*

Mom had me meet her at Bloomie's (I wasn't cut off then!) where she bought me the best mattress on the market. She also splurged and bought me a down-filled mattress pad, five-hundred-thread sheets, a quilt for summer, a feather-stuffed comforter for winter, shams, bolsters and a white linen duvet. Before Mom and I went shopping, I didn't even know what shams, bolsters and duvets were. Now, I live to lie down on them. My bed is a beautiful cumulus cloud that I rarely want to leave.

'Susanna!'

It's just before ten on Saturday morning and I've had a long week as Nell's servant. Mom's voice echoes through the whole apartment. She calls out, 'You gonna sleep all day?'

Frankly, I'm considering it. It's my day off, after all. Being Nell's errand girl is strenuous. And my bed *is* heavenly. I dreamed I lived on a ledge in the Himalayas with a Sherpa who provides luxury bedding. And the Sherpa looks freakishly like Brad Pitt.

'Susanna *Marie.*' Mom makes my name sound like an incurable disease. I cover my head with a sham.

The headboard on my bed is utterly amazing, too. It's made of chocolate-coloured wood with pearly beading around the edges. I found it on Park Avenue in a mongo raid. In fact, that's how I've decorated my entire room. Whenever I need something, um, *new*, Amelia comes with me. We get up early on garbage day, take the L-train to Union Square, transfer to the uptown number six, get off at East Sixty-Eighth, walk over to Park and start 'shopping' for *mongo,* i.e. recycled garbage. Hey, one girl's trash is another's treasure.

The doormen all know us by now.

'Want an oak credenza?' one whispered a couple of months ago, as Amelia and I walked past.

'Sure!' I said, not that I had a clue what a credenza was. But my heart leaped when the doorman led me to a gorgeous wood cabinet. Amelia liked it too. A small chunk of wood was chipped off the corner, and the drawer didn't open – but what's perfect? The doorman even helped Amelia and me carry it back to Sixty-Sixth Street and lift it onto the cross-town bus.

Mom was mortified. 'How do you know a dog hasn't peed on it?'

Why is everyone obsessed with dog waste? Though, it's not an unreasonable question. Even Park Avenue dogs pee on garbage. So, each time I bring something home, I scrub it down with some urine neutraliser like Nature's Miracle. Still, I suspect my mother's objection to my furniture 'recycling' has more to do with style than any canine contribution. My parents' decorating taste can best be described as 'Ikea Chic'. It's all blond wood and simple lines and washable. They can't see the beauty in mongo.

We live in a 'penthouse' apartment. Which – as I'm beginning to feel about my internship – sounds better than it is. Actually, it's the top floor of an old five-storey building in the meat-packing district. It's a cool neighbourhood now, but when my parents moved here, before I was born, there were more sides of beef hanging around than residents. Unless you count the transvestites who hung out on the playground across the street. (They still hang out here, but now call themselves 'gender dysphorics' and buy their humungous girl-shoes at Daffy's, on Fifth.)

Even though a lot of the meat-carcass warehouses are gone, they're not *all* gone. There's definitely a rotting meat aroma on hot summer days. Which takes a lot of the chic out of our 'hood.

Once, during a heat wave, Dad told me it smelled like a busy day at the morgue, which must *really* put a dent in our property values. And, yesterday, before I could leave my building, I had to shoo a rat away from the front door. It wasn't easy. He looked at me like, 'Hey, I was here first.' He definitely had an attitude.

'Susanna Marie Barringer!'

I know my mother. She won't give up until I get up. And I've run out of names.

Rolling out of bed, I slap my bare feet across the hardwood floor and join my mother in the kitchen.

'Good morning, Mother,' I say sweetly.

'You're up,' she says.

I roll my eyes.

'I'm taking the boys to the river,' Mom says. 'It's lovely out. Why don't you come with us?'

Strands of sunlight are darting through the rusted-metal fire escape that butts up against our living room window. Even though I'm seriously tempted to crawl back onto my cushy Himalayan ledge, I choose the karmically-correct route.

'Okay, Mom. Give me a minute to get dressed.'

If I help my mother today with my three one-year-old brothers, maybe the universe will help me bust out of menial servitude on Monday.

*

A strawberry smoothie is waiting for me on the kitchen counter. The Trips are 'packed'. Evan is playing with his toes, Henry is playing with Evan's hair, and Sam is (as usual) staring into space.

'Don't slouch, Susanna,' Mom says. 'Shoulders on a hanger!'

I stand up straight, imagine my shoulders are hanging in my closet.

'That's better,' Mom says. 'Now, hurry up.' I smell her sunscreen, see the worry crease in her forehead. If we don't get to the river soon, one of the boys will fuss. Once one goes, it's a domino effect. The curse of thirteen-month-old triplets.

'Go on ahead,' I say. 'I'll catch up.'

Mom gives me a look.

'I'll catch up. I swear.'

She nods, rolls the triple-decker stroller down the hall and out the front door.

'See you soon, sweetie,' I hear her yell, recognising the edge in my Mom's voice. Her 'see you soon, sweetie' is as much of a command as a farewell. The elevator lands on the fifth floor with a *clunk.* Thank God it's working today.

For the first fourteen years and two months of my life, it was just my parents and me (and, of course, my imaginary celebrity friends). At the time, I didn't appreciate it for the glorious time it was. I was the queen in my own family, but didn't understand its power until it was gone.

In desperation – and probably using my (non-ivy-league)

college fund – Mom had IVF and *poof*! I didn't have one sibling, I had three. My parents were stunned, too.

From the moment my brothers were born, our family focus has been on three wriggling spit-up machines. I was pretty much left alone before my brothers were born; now, I'm invisible. Unless Mom needs me to help.

Don't get me wrong. I love having brothers. But *three* at once? You have no idea how much a family can change overnight. Our apartment looks like a Toys R Us store after a clearance sale. No matter how many times we clean it up, The Trips mess it up.

Also, my parents decided to arrange their schedules so they could raise the triplets without a nanny. Why? Because they figured they already had live-in help: me. After The Trips were born, I stopped being a daughter and became a babysitter. My parents are majorly stressed out. Mom's favourite phrase is 'hurry up', and Dad's is 'Susanna, can you run to Duane Reade and buy more Pampers?'

I'm not completely heartless. After my smoothie, I speed-walk toward Hudson River Park and catch up with my mom before she crosses the West Side Highway. I blow Henry's nose and pull a Cheerio out of Evan's. I feel sorry for my mom. She tries to be the perfect parent, but she definitely got more than she bargained for. Most of the time, she seems like she's sleepwalking.

Once we get to the river walk, Mom plops down on a park bench and wearily leans against the back of it.

'Anything interesting happen at school last week, Susanna?' she asks, resting her eyes for a moment.

'It's *summer*, Mom,' I say.

'Oh yeah. That's right. It's summer.'

NINE

My mouth is dry. I have no idea what I'm in for. Carmen is escorting me to meet Sasha in The Closet.

'You look like you're on your way to prison,' she says. 'You should be happy.'

'Why?' I ask. 'What's in The Closet?'

'What's in The Closet?!' Carmen speeds up and I scamper behind her.

When we get to the fashion department, Sasha is waiting outside a locked door, dangling a key between her thumb and forefinger.

'Ready?' she asks.

I try to swallow. 'I guess so.'

Carmen smiles as Sasha inserts the key and opens the door to a *room.* It isn't a closet at all, though it's lined from floor to ceiling with stuff.

'Welcome to the most coveted spot in publishing,' Sasha says. 'The fashion closet.'

Inside, my jaw drops. I'm standing in the middle of what can only be called a fashion *wonderland.* I'm surrounded by thousands (millions?) of dollars of clothes, shoes, handbags, scarves, earrings . . . you name it. Three walls are lined with racks. All the racks are colour-coded – red clothes hang together, as do blues, blacks, stripes, sequins. It's a rainbow of designer duds. The fourth wall is stacked from floor to ceiling with shoes. I've never seen more spiked heels. Who can walk on those things? A large white cushioned chair sits in the corner. In the centre, a huge rectangular table full of handbags and jewellery sparkles like a giant kaleidoscope.

'Fabulous, isn't it?' Sasha says.

I nod, relieved. Sasha is going to make me over!

'Enjoy yourselves,' Carmen says. As she walks away, Sasha shuts the door and says to me, 'Take off your clothes. I only have a few minutes.'

'Undress?' I ask. 'Right here?'

'How *else* do you try on clothes?' she asks, impatiently.

Of course, this makes perfect sense, though it doesn't make me feel any less exposed. Under my breath, I pray that I'm wearing my prettiest pants. I was running late, so I grabbed the first pair in my drawer that morning without really looking. As I inhale, I feel my bra. I *think* it's the new one with the satin bow, not (please, God) my comfy old sports bra with the sweat stains.

Sasha is busy flipping through clothes. I hear her say, 'No, no, no, *God* no,' which flattens my confidence a bit. Still, I hang my shoulders on a hanger and unbutton the pink cotton shirt Mom bought me at Target.

Scene's fashion closet, Sasha explains while she flips

through the clothes, is nothing compared to *Vogue*'s or *Elle*'s. They have more of a fashion *floor*. After all, we cover celebrities mostly, and they wear what they wear. But, in every issue, *Scene* has at least one fashion piece. Like, 'Who's Hot . . . and Who's a Designer Dud?' Or, 'How To Create A Star's Style From Your Own Closet'. Because of this, clothes pour in from every designer in New York and Paris. Some let us keep the clothes.

'The designers we like,' Sasha says.

Some make us give the clothes back even if we use them in a shoot.

'The designers we never use again,' adds Sasha, laughing.

All the clothes that stay – shoes, hats . . . *everything* – go into the closet. Sasha and Nell hold the only two keys.

'You're about a size fourteen?' Sasha asks me, as I stand there in my (thankfully!) new bra.

'Ten,' I say.

Actually, I'm sometimes a size twelve. And one time, the Capri pants I bought at Costco were a very snug twelve. But, I had my mom return them. Clearly, they were defective.

'I'm tall,' I say to Sasha, like that has to do with anything. Models are six-feet tall and a size *six*.

'Try this.'

She hands me a narrow black skirt with a slit up the side. My heart sinks. I *know* I'll never get my butt into that.

'I prefer flared,' I say, lamely. 'I love elastic waists.'

Sasha just stands there. 'Try it.'

It's a little cold standing there in my bra. And I'm not looking forward to disrobing completely. Even at home, I dress one half before I undress the other.

'Any shirts in there?' I ask, glancing at the rack of purples. I love purple!

Sasha says, 'I need to see how the skirt looks first.'

My shoulders slip off their hanger a bit, but I take a deep breath and pull down the elastic-waist, flared skirt I'm wearing. To my utter mortification, my pants are ripped at the thigh. They're pink, too. With tiny flowers. Like I'm eleven-years-old.

'I was late this morning,' I squeak.

Sasha shifts her weight onto her other hip and sighs.

I've never felt more naked in my life. Even though I'm not naked at all. Most bikinis are smaller than my girly pants and bra. Still, I feel like I'm at the doctor's office and he's about to do a pelvic exam. Why are the lights in here so bright?

Quickly, I step out of my skirt and into the black skirt Sasha gave me. Even as I pull it up, I know there's no hope. It barely makes it past my knees.

'It's a little snug,' I say.

'Yes,' Sasha says, simply. Then she turns around and continues to flip through the racks. 'No, no, no, *God* no.'

Sasha hands me another skirt – a bit shorter, without a slit. This one makes it up to my thighs. She then tosses trousers my way, two button-front dresses, a plaid skirt with pleats. No, no, *God* no. The white chair in the corner soon becomes buried with the damning evidence that the Costco Capris probably weren't defective after all.

My nooks and crannies are very damp. What began as a thrilling invitation, is quickly morphing into the most humiliating afternoon of my life. I find myself wishing it *was* a pelvic exam. At least you're eventually allowed to put your clothes back on and leave. As Sasha makes her way around the room, she periodically hands me something else to squeeze into. This time, it's a white dress with an empire waist.

'Who's fat under their boobs?' Sasha asks, when I can't zip it up.

Of course, it soon becomes painfully clear that the fashion closet is for *models*, the aforementioned six-footers who wear size six. A fifteen-year-old girl who had two bowls of Cheerios that morning – I got caught in an endless cycle of adding a few more Cheerios at the end to soak up the excess milk, then adding more milk to mix with the excess Cheerios – will only find humiliation here. I also find myself feeling incredibly hungry, which must be a psychological need to fill the gaping hole in my self-confidence.

'What size are your feet?' Sasha asks.

Finally! Something to be proud of!

'Tiny,' I say, confidently. I've always been proud that my feet could probably fit into Cinderella's glass slipper.

'Crap.' Sasha's hands fall from her hips to her thin thighs.

'What's wrong?'

'Models have huge feet.'

'What about these?'

Before Sasha can stop me, I grab a pair of strappy sandals that look like they might fit my unmodel-sized feet. I throw one foot in, grab one of the straps, pull and feel a *snap*.

'Oops,' I say, holding a dangling broken strap in my hand.

Sasha's eyes bug out of her head. 'That's a four-hundred-dollar pair of Manolo Blahniks!' she shrieks.

Sasha then marches to the accessories table, grabs three scarves, a few pairs of dangly earrings, and a heavy handbag that has chains and buckles all over it. I hate them all.

'Thanks,' I say.

'It's the best I can do.'

Before she stomps out of the closet on a sparkly gold pair of four-inch heels, Sasha grabs my pink claw clip, squeezes it, and pulls it out of my hair.

'Never wear this again,' she says, throwing it on the floor and crushing it under her foot. 'Make sure the door is locked when you leave.'

With that, my makeover comes to an abrupt end. Sasha storms out, leaving me standing there in my ripped underwear, staring at the broken pieces of the only claw clip I have that perfectly matches my pink fake-leather shoes.

TEN

It's Week Two. I've mastered the Starbucks run, the 'start' button on the Xerox machine, and Manhattan bus and subway routes. It's time to steal a few moments to do a little in-house reporting. After all, if I'm going to be a magazine mogul, I'd better know how a magazine works. Holding an empty teacup in case anyone asks me why I'm lurking about, I wander through the different departments of *Scene*.

'Brad sold well, but Jen was a sell-out,' I hear senior editor Renée say through her open office door. 'And everyone is bored beyond belief by Angelina's good works. Suggestions?'

'Ashton and Demi?'

'Yawn.'

'Benifer Two?'

'Barf. No one cares about Ben Affleck and his Jennifer obsession.'

'Is Cher dating anyone?'

'Cher? C'mon people! Are you brain-dead? I want three knockout cover couples on my desk by four o'clock. And three incredible cover lines. Nothing rhyming. I'm sick of rhymes. Be clever. Think *fresh*, think *new*, think *short.* Our readers have the attention span of a gnat. Don't tax their wee intellects! Now go, go, *go*!'

Who knew Renée was a mini Nell? Does she ask Francesca to check her body for bloat?

I continue meandering around the office and overhear snippets of phone conversations.

'What? You *promised*!'

'Yeah, yeah. What has he done *lately*?'

'Hey, is it *my* fault he was acquitted? The jury has their heads up their arses.'

The air is super-charged with tension. Even though we're supposedly in the 'calm' period of the publishing cycle, the editorial beehive is a-buzz. Someone bursts into tears in the middle of the cubicle maze. I hear her sob, 'Nell wouldn't give me time off to help my mom with my step-father's funeral. She said, "It's not like he was your *dad*".'

In another cubicle, a guy shrieks. 'I got the exclusive!'

The sobber stops sobbing and several heads poke up above the cubby walls.

'Who? Who? Who?'

I join the other 'owls'.

'Who?' I ask.

No one pays attention to me. They pop their heads back down and I never hear who will talk to *Scene* magazine and nobody else. But, as I continue walking, I *do* hear an editor dictate to his assistant.

'Best known for his signature sunglasses and intensely

poetic songwriting, the Irish singer is survived by his wife, Alison and childr—'

'Bono died?!' I dash over. 'Oh my God! What happened? When?'

Now, I'm almost sobbing.

The editor, a skinny guy in tinted blue glasses and pencil-thin black jeans, eyes me over the rim of his lenses.

'You are?' he asks.

'Nell's intern, Susanna. What happened to Bono?!'

'Ah yes, the high-school kid. Keep your panties on, Susanna. Bono is alive and well and probably saving starving children in Africa.'

'I thought I heard yo—'

'You did,' he says. Then he holds out his bony right hand for me to shake it. 'I'm Ricky. I write obits.'

'Obits?'

'Obituaries. You know, all the arse-kissing stuff they say about people when they die.'

'But you said Bono is alive,' I say.

'You don't think we wait till the last minute, do you?'

The empty teacup dangles in my hand. *Scene* magazine has a guy who writes obituaries for a living? Suddenly, scrutinising Nell Wickham's pores doesn't seem so bad.

Someone bumps me from behind. She says, 'Sorry,' as she scurries past, but it's just a casual toss over her shoulder. I can tell she isn't sorry at all. As I make my way back to my table – what name will Nell be calling me today? – I see a large colour photograph on the industrial grey carpet. Must have been dropped by the rude girl who isn't even slightly sorry she rammed into me. Bending down to pick it up, I notice that it's a candid shot of Drew Barrymore. Only, I can barely make her out, because the photo is marked up with a red waxy pencil. Several small red circles dot her face. A red line runs down her thigh; another one intersects the stripe of skin visible below her short halter top.

'There it is!'

Rude Girl returns and snatches the photo from my hands.

'Thanks,' she says, but I can tell she isn't thankful at all. She doesn't even look at me. Wheeling around on her ballet flats, she races back down the hall.

'Hey, wait a minute,' I call after her.

She stops. 'What?'

'What are all those red marks?'

Rude Girl rolls her eyes and says, 'You must be new.'

'I work with Nell,' I say, holding my head up, careful not to say *for* Nell or mention anything about bloat.

Clearly put-out, Rude Girl says, 'Her flaws are circled.'

'Flaws? It's Drew Barrymore.'

She clucks her tongue. 'Every celebrity has flaws – unless we digitally correct them. Really, do you think anyone looks as good in person as they do in a magazine?'

Well, yes, I had. Drew's skin is awesome. Or, do I just *think* it is? Bono isn't dead, and some criminal got off because the members of his jury have the incredible flexibility to insert their heads up their own butts. My head is spinning.

'They don't call Hollywood the Land of Make-Believe for nothing,' Rude Girl says. 'And who do you think pays the bills? If celebs don't look hot in our magazine, is anyone going to buy the products on the next page? We make our readers believe that they too can look like a star if they slather on our advertisers' creams or use their shampoos. It's all a total joke.'

With that, Rude Girl takes off in a blur of black. I stand there, contemplating my new view of the celebrity universe (does Jude Law have zits??) until another blur in black flies by and says, 'You're Sue, right?'

'Right,' I say. Why bother correcting anyone any more?

'Nell is screaming your name.'

ELEVEN

My parents are on a date. Which is really cute considering their last official 'date' was seventeen years ago, when my dad burst into tears at the end of *Dances With Wolves* and asked my mom to marry him right there in the movie theatre. On his knees and everything.

'*Goodfellas* was also playing that year,' Mom loves to joke. 'He almost asked me to be his gangster.'

The Trips are all fed, bathed and in their jammies. I've nestled the four of us in the centre of a pillow cloud on my bed. Henry is in one arm, Evan in the other. Sam is propped up between my crossed legs. Amazingly, they've stopped wriggling long enough to hear a bedtime story. But, they smell like baby powder and shampoo, and look so adorable it's impossible to stop kissing them long enough to read Dr Seuss.

Already, my brothers have distinct personalities. Evan is playful, Henry is mischievous, and Sam is introspective. Even now, I see their individuality emerge. Evan has his foot in his mouth, Henry is quietly trying to push Sam off the bed, and Sam is wistfully staring at *The Cat in the Hat.*

My cell rings. It's Mel.

'I can't talk now,' I say, barely holding my phone between my shoulder and ear. 'I'm babysitting The Trips.'

'Need help?' she asks.

'Not at the moment. Thanks.'

'If you do, call me and I'll cab right over.'

I smile. That is *so* like Mel.

We've been best friends for ever. Well, almost. Ever since Mrs Merrick made us lab partners in seventh-grade life sciences class.

'Here's a list of the stuff we'll need to create our biosphere at the end of the semester,' Mel had said, handing me a typed page.

'The *end* of the semester? It's the first day of class.'

'I like to be prepared.'

Amelia confessed, 'Obsessive compulsiveness runs in my family.'

She wasn't kidding. If you put us together, you'll see that Mel and I are perfect opposites. I have blue eyes, she has brown. My curly brown hair is shoulder-length, parted down the middle; Mel's is dark, straight and short. I'm not *fat*, but I'm definitely not thin. Amelia isn't *anorexic*, but she's definitely skinny. I live on the lower west side, Mel lives in Chelsea. And, personality-wise, well, we couldn't be more different. Once, I even made a list.

AMELIA VS. SUSANNA

AMELIA	SUSANNA
Plans everything ahead of time, including her weekly school outfits.	Usually picks up whatever's on the floor to wear. Why not clean my room while I dress?
Refuses to even eat a snack before her homework is done.	Can't think, work, play or even eat without major food first.
Has been saving for Princeton since third grade.	Sincerely hope my parents have saved at least something for college. Too scared to ask.
Believes in the basic goodness of all human beings.	Hopes for basic goodness in all human beings.
Can laugh at herself, but often doesn't.	Can laugh at myself – and others – and often do.
Spends her day helping cancer patients.	Spend my day pondering the social implications of Botox. Will Hollywood eventually only make comedies because they can't find an actor with functioning frown lines?
Is the kindest, most thoughtful person I've ever met.	Is a great friend, a good daughter, an awesome girlfriend (if ever given the chance to prove it!), and someone who believes anything is possible if I try hard enough.

Sitting on my bed, I hang up my cell and watch three pairs of tiny eyelids slowly droop. Sam falls asleep first, then Evan, then – fighting to stay awake – Henry finally lets go. Gently, I lower them flat on my bed. I don't dare move them into their cribs. Not just yet. Instead, I look at my little brothers and think, I'm the luckiest girl in the world.

TWELVE

I don't believe it! It's him. I'm sure it's him. My heart races as I scurry east on Gansevoort Street in hot pursuit. The universe put another opportunity in front of me and I'm not going to squander it. I, Susanna Barringer, will soon snag an impromptu on-the-street interview with George Clooney. A scoop! I can't believe it! What luck! Nell Wickham will soon see she has hired a goldmine. My messenger days will be over.

He's wearing baggy cargo pants, a light grey T-shirt and sandals. Even from a block behind, I can see that he's gorgeous; better-looking than he is on television or in the movies. He's shorter, his hair is darker, too.

'Excuse me. Sorry. Pardon me. Oops. Was that your foot?'

It's the workday morning rush. Ninth Avenue is packed with people. I squeeze through the crowd as politely as possible, my eyes never leaving Gorgeous George. No one has recognised him yet, so he's not mobbed. He's just walking, like a regular guy, up a regular street. He crosses Thirteenth Street, and looks to the right. Is he headed for Union Square?

I brace myself to make a mad dash diagonally across the Avenue, but George keeps walking uptown at a fast clip until he turns right at the next block.

Even this early in the day, the humidity must be approaching one hundred per cent. The air feels so thick it might just burst into rain. Where is he going?

Already, I'm sweating so much my faux Tods are sliding off my feet. My hair looks like dreadlocks. I'm going to be late for work, but who cares? I *am* working! I'm about to land a 'teen perspective' interview with one of the few stars that *everybody* loves – teens and their parents, men and women. Keeping him in sight, I take a moment to compose a fabulous, insightful question. 'Who are you wearing?' isn't going to cut it with George Clooney. Clearly, he's clad in old Levis. Which is *so* George, isn't it? Why spend a fortune on clothes when you look as good as he does?

Like Brad, I decide to appeal to George's playful, impish side. I'll ask, 'If your prom date called you today, what would you talk about?' Then, I'll follow-up with a more hard-hitting question: 'What's the one thing you want her to know about you today?'

All of a sudden, George Clooney stops on Fourteenth. It's time to make my move. Now or never. I take a deep breath and quicken my pace. George Clooney gets closer. My heart beats faster. Just as I'm about to close in on my prey, he raises his tanned muscular arm and hails a cab.

A *cab*!? Why now? Did he sense me behind him?

Brakes creak as a cab stops, and George Clooney – my future career – hops in.

'Taxi!' I shriek, flapping my arm like a windshield-wiper gone berserk. Another cab stops and I leap into the back seat. 'Follow that cab!' I shout. The driver looks out the window, then back at me.

'Which one?' he asks in a heavy Middle-Eastern accent.

I see his point. Fourteenth Street is one long yellow stripe of bumper-to-bumper taxis. Why would George Clooney take a cab in this traffic? A two-toed sloth could move faster.

'That one,' I say, pointing to George's cab. At least, he hasn't got away. I see the back of his studly head through the rear window.

'As you wish,' my driver says. With horns honking, pedestrians making obscene gestures at us, and my body lurching forward each time the driver jerks farther into the next lane, we finally get into position three cabs behind George's.

'Good, good. Keep going,' I say. My driver seems to need encouragement. He keeps turning his head around and lifting his caterpillar eyebrows at me.

'You're doing great,' I say. 'We're on his tail.'

Every few minutes, I pull another dollar out of my wallet. I want to be ready to pay *fast* if George Clooney decides to exit his cab at a red light. Already, the meter has clicked past five bucks. Even though the back seat is air-conditioned, I'm sweating more than I was on the street. What if George is cabbing it to the FDR Drive? Or worse, the *airport*? He can afford to sit in a taxi all afternoon. Me? I quickly look through my wallet. Hopefully, George Clooney isn't going farther than Park Avenue because the east side is the end of my cash. Had I known I'd be inching across town with the meter running, I never would have spent *any* money on *Ass*-trid's stupid blueberry muffin.

We continue toward the East River, past Whole Foods and a gazillion banks. Suddenly, my cab driver jams on the brakes.

'He pull over,' he says, excitedly. 'You want me pull over, too?'

George Clooney's cab has stopped at the curb. I see his door swing open.

'Yes!' I screech, tossing the seven dollars I have ready in my hand into the front seat. Then I apologise for throwing money at the driver and thank him for his help. My driver beams and says, 'Good luck to catch your man!'

George Clooney is not far ahead on the crowded sidewalk. Apparently, he figured he could walk faster than a cab can drive. (Which, at the moment, is true.) He's still heading east. This time, I won't let him get away.

My heart rate speeds up again. I frantically fish through my bag for a pen to jot down his responses. Quickly, I devise a game plan. I'll get directly behind him, wait for a red light, then leap in front and fire my first question at him. That way, he won't have time to compose a bland movie star answer. I will catch him being *himself*. He will smile, admire my guts, and launch my teenage butt into the big time.

Up ahead, the light turns yellow. George slows. Zigzagging through the crowd, I catch up to him. Heart thumping, I shut my eyes and go for it.

'Hey, George!' I leap into the gutter, whip around, open my eyes, and ask, 'If your prom date called you today, what would you talk about?'

My heart is practically pummelling George Clooney in the chest, we are so crammed together. And, my plan is perfect. He *does* look startled. Horrified, in fact. There's only one problem: up close and personal, I realise with sickening clarity that the man I've been following for the sweaty past half-hour isn't George Clooney at all. He's just a regular guy, on a regular street, in an old pair of Levis.

'I . . . I don't know,' the guy answers in response to my searing celebrity question. 'I didn't go to my prom.' Then, as if I care, he says, thoughtfully, 'I always wished I had. Funny, the things you regret.'

Regret? I know all about regret. What made me think George Clooney had black hair? And big ears? Did I really think George Clooney would wear flip-flops in New York City? Had I lost my mind?

Suddenly, I freeze. Is it possible that George Clooney's great looks are *digital*? Peering intensely at the man on the street, I decide, no. This is definitely *not* Gorgeous George. I've seen every rerun of *ER*. No one would digitally alter a television show, would they? If they did, wouldn't they give Anthony Edwards more hair?

Forcing a smile, I nod and let not-George go. Shoulders sagging completely off their hanger, I realise that my *biggest* regret is now being downtown on the east side, with three bucks in my wallet, and only fifty cents on my MetroCard. As the sun sizzles above me, I wonder why, today of all days, did I wear black?

THIRTEEN

'Nell's looking for you,' *Ass*-trid says to me, the moment I step off the elevator. 'I told her you overslept.'

'What?!'

'You're welcome.'

Everyone stares at me as I run through the editorial bullpen. Someone says, 'Nell is on the warpath,' and I can tell that everyone knows I'm in trouble. Their mouths puff out with pity while their eyes sparkle with glee.

'That's her?' I hear someone whisper. 'No wonder.'

Nell is in the middle of the morning editorial meeting. Still, I burst into her office, heaving.

'You're looking for me?' I say, way too loud.

'Nice of you to pop by,' Nell says, her voice dripping in icicles. Today, she wears red.

'I was—' I start to explain the George Clooney fiasco, but I think twice. If I can't even identify a bonafide celebrity, how will she ever trust me?

'I overslept,' I say.

'Don't do it again,' Nell says. And that's it. She turns to

face the group of editors in her office, and Carmen quietly rises and gets me a chair.

As I sit there, trying to catch my breath, it dawns on me that I'm sitting in the *Scene* magazine editorial meeting. Power Central. The room where decisions are made. What are people talking about this week? Who will be on the cover? Anyone's marriage on the rocks this week? Any movie premieres to attend?

All the main editors are there – Sasha, Renée and (sigh) Keith. Today he wears camouflage pants with black boots and a tight black T-shirt. His hair is loose, and I can barely look at him without drooling.

Suddenly, Nell turns to me and says, 'Now that you're finally here, Susan, we can probe that teenage mind of yours.'

My heart skips. Oh my God! It's happening. Right here and now. Finally, my real career is about to begin!

My tongue feels like an old sock. I'm finding it hard to inhale.

'Chill,' I say to myself. 'Breathe.'

Breathing in and out, I will my heart to stop racing. What am I so worried about? I'm *ready.* In preparation for this moment, I'd composed a list of riveting, magazine-worthy, Nell-dazzling teen topics.

- HOOKING UP: What does the girl get out of it?
- COMMUNITY SERVICE: Just another attempt to keep us off the streets?

- ABSTINENCE-ONLY SEX ED: Will adults ever get real?
- ATTENTION SUV OWNERS! Gas-guzzling, smog-producing, oil-dependent road hogs do not make you look hot!

Or, if those are too political, I'm ready with *celebrity* topics, too.

- BRITNEY BACKLASH: Does anyone care about Britney and Kevin?
- Are Benecio del Toro and Brad Pitt really father and son?
- If Josh Hartnett offered to be your first, would you still just say no?
- REALITY TV: Whose Reality? Not mine!

I sit up straight, hang my shoulders on a hanger. Finally, I'll be able to stop being Nell's servant, and start spreading my journalistic wings. At long last, I'll be able to soar in the thrilling world of publishing.

'Probe away, Nell,' I say, flipping my hair casually. 'I happen to have a few ideas of my own to toss in.'

'Are you a virgin?' she asks.

'Excuse me?'

'A *virgin*?' She pronounces the word with an 'h'. *Veh*-gin.

I try not to blush, you know, the way a total *veh*-gin would. But it's no use. My cheeks flare instantly. I can feel Keith's eyes on me even as I study my lap.

'Well, yes,' I mutter. 'As a matter of fact, I am.'

'Brilliant!' Nell claps her hands together. 'We were hoping you were.'

Hoping? Mortified, I realise that my virginity was the topic of conversation in the meeting. Maybe even the whole office! Did *anyone* think I might *not* be one? Did they take a vote? An inter-office memo? No way will I ever be able to look at Keith Franklin again. My neck begins to flush, too. I can feel itchy red spots explode like fireworks.

'As a *veh*-gin, then,' Nell says, 'who would you say is your favourite actor? Your heart-throb.'

That's easy.

'Randall Sanders,' I blurt out, trying to ignore my burning cheeks. I've been in love with him for ever . . . since I first saw him in the made-for-TV movie, *Search for a Serial Strangler*. And he turned out to be the serial strangler! Randall Sanders just does that to you. Not only is he a fantastic actor, he's an awesome guy you can't help dreaming about. After the strangler movie, he bought his mom a house. Who doesn't love a guy who buys his mom a house with his first big paycheck? Even a guy who terrorises the entire city of Los Angeles with a phone cord!

Now, Randall Sanders is the hottest man in Hollywood. Though, who could be surprised? His mink-brown eyes peer straight into your soul. And that sandy blond hair – well, I don't know how he does it, but it's always *perfectly* mussed. He never looks messy. It's the difference between wanting to give him a comb and a kiss. A *major* kiss.

Nell nods. 'I can see that,' she says.

Sasha and Renée nod, too. Keith may be nodding, but no way can I look at him yet. Not with my (non) sexual status fresh on his mind.

'Okay then. That's all, Anna,' Nell says, dismissing me with a wave of her hand.

That's all? And, I'm *Anna* now?

Before I leave the room, Sasha shouts, 'I'm calling in some larger clothes. It may take a while.'

The staff bursts out laughing and I slink away – an outed virgin, with a crush on Randall Sanders and Keith Franklin, and a size that's frighteningly close to my age. No, my summer adventure isn't going well at all.

FOURTEEN

Our new weekly ritual: Amelia and I meet for a drink after work. That's what we call it, anyway, to sound cool. In reality, I take the subway to Ninety-Sixth Street, walk over to Fifth and meet Mel in the cafeteria at Mount Sinai Hospital, where she's getting a jump on next year's community service. She's a volunteer in the Palliative Care Unit.

'The *huh*?' I'd asked, when I first heard the name.

'It's where terminal patients go for pain management,' she'd explained.

'You mean, like, patients who are going to die?'

'Yeah. Exactly like that.'

Can you imagine anything more depressing? But, Mel swears it's not.

'You can't believe how full of life they are,' she'd said.

We meet for a lemonade.

'Sugar-free, please,' I say, as we move through the cafeteria line. Usually I get a cookie, too. But not today. Not until my size stops being a teenager.

Lemonades in hand (mine made with Splenda ... *brilliant*!) we sit at a table near the window.

'What's new in *Celebrityville*?' Mel asks, draping a napkin over the lap of her pink hospital smock. I decide to skip telling my best friend about The Outing. Amelia would go all volcanic and insist I file a sex discrimination lawsuit. Or, more accurately, a *no*-sex suit. Besides, I have lots of other stories to share.

'Nell asked me if she looks like Halle Berry,' I say.

'Does she?'

'Hmmm. Let's see. She has white-blonde hair, she's pale to the point of looking bloodless, and she's as thin and shapeless as a pencil – yeah, I'd say so.'

Mel laughs. I stand, lean across the table and, in my best British accent, say, 'Could you look up my nose, *dah*ling, and tell me if you see any boogers?'

'Your boss has self-esteem issues. Or, at least she needs self-esteem *tissues*.'

We both laugh hard at that one.

Amelia says, 'There's a guy upstairs I want you to meet.'

'A guy?' My heart starts thudding. Why didn't I wash my hair that morning?! The top is all flat! My parting is greasy!

'His name is Edgar,' she says.

'Edgar?' I picture the Computer Club President. Or, a tuba player in the high-school band. Not that I can afford to be picky, with my (now public!) terminal virgin status.

'Is Edgar also a volunteer?' I ask.

'He's cool,' Mel says. 'You'll see.'

The air in the Palliative Care Unit smells of stale flower water and disinfectant. I hear the hum of fluorescent lights, and the *squeak, squeak* of the nurses' rubber-soled shoes as they stride up and down the halls. Mel leads me straight into one of the patients' rooms.

'Hey, Eddie!' she says, cheerfully.

A pale, severely wrinkled old man puts his book down. He peers at us over reading glasses.

'Is that my angel, Amelia?'

'*Two* angels. I've brought my best friend, Susanna, to meet you.'

I glare at Mel. Is this her idea of a joke? Edgar is a thousand years old, and so tiny, you can barely see his form beneath the sheets. He has a tube in his nose, and one in his arm. Uneasy, I stay close to the door.

'I'm not contagious,' Edgar says, 'I'm only dying.'

Amelia laughs. I freeze. She says, 'It's okay, Susanna. Eddie is awesome.'

I've never been this close to a sick person, much less someone who's about to check out. Two of my grandparents died before I was born. The other two are alive and living in Maine. They wear cable-knit sweaters and hoist lobster pots up from the Gulf near their house. Every time I see them, they seem more alive than my worn-out parents.

Edgar asks Amelia, 'Is she a mute?'

'Sorry,' I stammer, as I step forward and shake Edgar's bony hand. 'Nice to meet you.'

'See?' he says, 'You didn't dissolve in a puff of smoke . . . yet.'

We stay with Edgar almost half an hour. Amelia is right. He's awesome.

'The only thing I'm sure about in life,' he says, 'is that when you're old, you have less hair where you want it, and more hair where you don't. I'm hoping for a deeper insight before I croak.'

Amazingly, I laugh. When Amelia first told me that her summer job would be hanging out with terminal patients who were all alone, I thought she was crazy. Not that staring up Nell's nose is sane. But, the last thing I expected was to – literally – laugh in the face of a man who will never leave his hospital bed.

'There's an old Tibetan saying,' Edgar says, '"When you're born, you cry and the world is joyous. When you die, the world cries and you are joyous." What a load of crap!'

A nurse stops by to check his blood pressure. A few minutes later, a doctor pops in and flips open Eddie's chart.

'Is he still giving you a hard time?' the doctor asks Amelia.

Mel smiles and says, 'I can take it. So far.'

When an orderly brings his dinner, Edgar asks him, 'Ever notice that the quality of hospital food deteriorates as fast as hospital fees go up? It's a conspiracy to get us the hell out of here as soon as possible. But the joke's on you. I'll be here the rest of my life.'

Like I said, I'm amazed at how much this frail little man can make me laugh.

Edgar, I find out, was a pharmacist in the West Village before he got sick. He worked six days a week, for the past thirty-seven years. 'If you really want to know people,' he says to me, 'look at the stuff they buy. You can't hide your true self in a drug store.'

I think about the truckload of Pampers I buy at Duane Reade each week, and my recent purchase of self-tanning cream. What does that say about me? I'm a teenage mother who longs to hang out at Jones' Beach? Come to think of it, after a day of babysitting The Trips, that's exactly how I feel.

Occasionally, Edgar presses a push-button he holds in his hand. It's attached to one of the tubes in his arm. He pushes the button, closes his eyes for a moment, breathes in and out, then opens his eyes and continues with the conversation.

'Tell me, Susanna,' he says, opening his eyes, 'what's it like to be you?'

I'm dumbfounded. How do you answer a question like that?

Edgar says, 'It's okay. I promise to take your secret to my grave.'

Again, I laugh. Though I really don't have an answer. Not one I can put into words, anyway. Being me, is like being weather. I'm stormy, hazy, sunny, breezy, cloudy; a flash flood when you least expect it. And, the weather predictions are always wrong. Who can say how weather will react?

'Come close,' Edgar says, suddenly serious. I think, Oh, no, he's not going to ask how his pores look, is he? Mel and I lean in.

Pressing the button in his hand again, Edgar takes a deep breath. He shuts his eyes so long it seems like he's asleep. Then, his eyes open slowly and he says, 'As soon as you figure out who you are, never be anyone else.'

FIFTEEN

I wake up to the sound of a balloon popping. My brothers are giggling hysterically. Mom and Dad are singing. 'When the moon is in the seventh house . . .'

'What's going on?'

My hair a flattened jumble of curls, I slap my bare feet into the kitchen. Through the sleep goo in my eyes, I see colourful balloons bobbing on the living-room ceiling. A lopsided cake sits on the coffee table. Three tiny toilets are arranged in a circle in the centre of the room. My three brothers, naked, sit on the toilets, clapping their tiny hands.

'We're having a potty party!' Mom says, adjusting her pointy hat.

Have *all* the adults in my life gone mad?

'It's the latest thing,' Dad says, catching Sam just before he topples off his potty.

'Shouldn't their toilets be in, oh, I don't know, the *bathroom*?' I ask.

'That's not how you do it,' Mom explains. 'First, you have to make peeing fun!'

She claps her hands and sings another hippie song from

the Sixties. My brothers can't stop smiling. They can't stop toppling over, either.

'Aren't they too young to be toilet-trained?' I ask, having read the book my parents thrust at me when The Trips were born. It outlined what to expect in the first few years of life. I remember groaning all the way through it.

Dad glances at Mom and they both sigh. 'We're trying it a tad early,' Mom says. 'Do you have any idea how expensive diapers are?'

Henry squeals. Dad's eyes light up and he lifts him up to check the toilet.

'False alarm,' he says, dejected, replacing my brother's butt on his potty.

As I watch my parents, I have to laugh. Is this much different than Nell staying up till dawn trying to pee out her margarita salt?

Popping a pointy hat on my head, I sit on the floor next to my parents. I grab Sam before he falls off his potty. Henry reaches over and tries to push Evan off his. We sing songs, clap our hands, bop balloons in the air. After about half an hour, we all give up and eat cake.

SIXTEEN

Truthfully, my stellar summer opportunity is beginning to look like a black hole. Thirty-three-and-a-third per cent of my summer is almost over and I'm about as close to being a celebrity-reporter as I am to wearing a model's clothes. Nell has an inexplicable fear of Fed Ex. They're *professionals* and still, she asks me to deliver stuff all over town. *Ass*-trid practically barfs on me every morning, Renée – the senior editor – ignores me entirely, and Keith Franklin looks at me like I'm his little sister. He even tousled my hair the other day, leaving it looking *messy,* not the slightest bit sexy.

I sigh. I groan. I find myself making all kinds of unhappy noises.

Today, I'm wearing a green skirt from Banana Republic, a white T, and one of the designer scarves that Sasha gave me from the fashion closet. It flies up in my face each time I walk faster than a slug. Which is rare. I've begun to *feel* like a slug each day at work – a fat, squishy slug surrounded by beautiful size-zero butterflies. How can a slug hang her shoulders on a hanger? She doesn't have shoulders!

On my desk – I mean, *table* – a giant stack of papers leans precariously, like the Tower of Pisa. Yellow Post-It Notes stick out from all sides. Each Post-It contains a command:

Copy and deliver ASAP.

Copy and give to Renée ASAP.

Copy and file. Return copy to Nell ASAP.

I moan. Can you go blind from staring at a copier light?

Francesca rushes past me. I smile at her and she says, 'You should try those new White Strips, Sue. Do you drink a lot of coffee?'

My hand flies up to my mouth.

One of the guys from the art department dashes past me and says, 'Someone needs a manicure!'

Sluggishly, I melt into my chair. At that exact moment, my phone rings.

'Hello?'

'Susanna?'

'Yes?'

'It's Willow.'

'Willow?'

'From Starbucks.'

'Oh yes,' I say. 'Hi, Willow. I don't need anything. Nell just had tea. And she's off carbs at the moment.'

'That's not why I'm calling,' Willow says quietly. I hear that she's at work. Shouted coffee orders – *venti skim latte!* – are audible in the background.

'Francesca said I should call you,' Willow whispers.

'She did?' Instantly, I feel anger rise in my sluggy chest. Tampons are one thing, but coffee? Francesca can get her own coffee!

'Look, Willow, I work for Ne—'

'Francesca told me about your nightmare in the fashion closet.' I gulp. 'There's no shame in being a size fourteen,' she says. 'Most of America is a size *fourteen* or over.'

'I'm not a *fourteen*,' I say, defensively. Then I lie. 'I'm an eight.'

'Ah.' I can hear that she doesn't believe me. Which really ticks me off. What business is it of hers anyway? Even if I was a *sixteen*, wouldn't she still have to make coffee for my boss? And *Francesca*! She *really* makes me mad! Why tell Willow anything at all? Especially that I'm a size fourteen when I'm really a size ten – most of the time. (Right after my period. On a good month.) And Sasha! What, she told the whole *world* about my mortification in The Closet?! Did she tell everyone about my ripped underwear, too?

Just as I'm about to explode, Willow whispers, 'I know about the Dolce Gabbanas.'

'Huh?'

'Francesca told me the fall line came in today.'

'So?'

'So –' I hear Willow move away from the latte orders. 'I was wondering . . . since you can't fit into them anyway, could you, maybe, score a dress for me?'

'What?' I can't believe my ears.

'Francesca said you might go for it.'

'Francesca was wrong,' I say.

'I'll give you all the free frappacinos you can drink. Extra whipped cream!'

I'm so mad, I want to whip her cream! The nerve!

'Number one,' I say to Willow, 'Nell is totally fine with me putting as many frappacinos – or anything else I want – on her account.'

I'm not sure about this, but I'm pretty sure Nell would prefer paying for my coffee than giving away clothes.

'Number two,' I continue, gathering steam, 'I don't *like* whipped cream. It tastes like thick air. And number three – Francesca got it wrong. Lots of clothes in The Closet fit me. I just don't want to look like a mortician when I'm come to work. I have my *own* style. Got it?'

Willow doesn't say a word.

'*Got* it?' I repeat.

'I was just asking, Susanna,' she says. 'You don't have to get all hysterical.'

'I'm not hysterical,' I say. 'I'm *busy.* I have a very important job at *Scene* magazine and Nell Wickham is waiting for me.'

As I slam the phone down, I feel shoulders sprout in my mushy body. I hold my head up. Enough is enough. As soon as I'm finished going blind at the Xerox machine, I'm going to shove my flapping scarf out of my face and let Francesca know there's a new Susanna – not Sue, Susan, Susie or Anna – at *Scene* magazine. It's time to grab hold of my destiny and show everyone that this slug is no slouch!

SEVENTEEN

'Suzanne! Join us!'

Eventually, I figure, Nell will run out of variations on my name and stumble on the right one.

The daily editorial meeting is in progress. For the second time in my, uh, *career,* Nell invites me into the inner circle. My stomach lurches, but I'm able to quickly calm it. Taking a deep breath, I say to myself: Susanna, it's time to make your mark. Even if Nell asks, 'How does it feel to be a fat teenage cow?' it's time to slip in a few ideas for the future *Teen Scene* magazine.

'Speaking of fat teenage cows,' I'll say, 'Why don't we do an exposé on how Hollywood breeds teenage anorexia?' Then I'll look directly at Francesca and say, 'What do you think? Were *you* inspired to stop eating by what you saw on TV?'

I'm going to show Nell – and everyone else – that I'm more than just a messenger. I, too, have the makings of a bitchy budding reporter. If that's what it takes to succeed, that's what I'll do.

As before, Nell sits in a soft white chair in her bright white office. Renée and Sasha are on the white couch to her right; Keith sits alone in the centre of the white couch to her left. Carmen sits beside Nell, holding a notepad. Francesca and the other assistant editors sit in chairs behind the far couch. She smiles a fake smile at me and I toss an even faker one right back at her.

'Hello everyone,' I say.

Sasha stands, strides over to me, and rearranges the scarf.

'It's not a necktie,' she says. After a few interminable seconds of fluffing and tying and untying, she rips it off my neck and says, 'You're hopeless.'

'Let's get started,' Nell says.

The only available seat is next to hunky Keith. If he'd move over. Which he doesn't. But I don't care. I'm no longer a slug. Brazenly, I march over to Keith's couch and lower my butt into the space next to his. I hold my designer scarf proudly in my lap.

'I'll have tea,' Nell says. 'Green. Organic.'

Keith looks at me. 'I'll have a cappuccino. Extra foam.'

Suddenly, the room erupts in coffee orders.

'Gingerbread latte, skim milk.'

'Caramel macchiato.'

'Iced Americano, two sugars.'

'Chai crème frappucino.'

I sink into the couch, dazed.

'Make that an *iced* gingerbread latte, will you, Sue?'

Nell asks, 'Can you remember all of this?'

I try to answer, but my lips are super-glued to my teeth.

Carmen, my knight*ess* in shining armour, stands and hands me her notepad with the coffee orders on it. 'Give her a moment to catch her breath,' she tells the thirsty crowd.

Mortified, I awkwardly lift myself out of the couch. The scarf flutters to the floor. I now understand why I was invited into the editorial meeting.

'An assortment of goodies would be *fabulous,* Susan,' Nell says. 'All sugar-free, of course. You might want to try that little food shop on the corner.'

I nod. Out of the corner of my eye, I see Francesca smirk.

'Is that it?' I ask, my voice squeaky.

'Yes. Hurry,' Nell commands.

Coffee orders in hand, I stoop to pick up my scarf, then slink out of the room. Abruptly, I stop.

'One more thing,' I say, turning around. My heart is pounding so hard my breast bone hurts. The scarf instantly gets wet in my hand. 'Francesca?'

Francesca's eyes go wide. The whole staff stares at me, waiting for me to speak, but I don't care. I feel suddenly empowered.

'Since I'm on my way to Starbucks,' I say, directly at her, ignoring Nell's impatient stare. 'Do you have any messages for Willow?'

Francesca swallows. 'No, thank you,' she says.

I say, 'Are you sure?'

She says, 'Yes.'

I say, 'Are you *sure*?'

Francesca's voice is a tiny echo at the bottom of her throat. 'Yes, I'm sure.'

'Susan,' Nell snaps, 'Have you gone mental?'

'No,' I reply, calmly. 'I know exactly what's going on.'

Glancing at Francesca one more time, I smile. This one is a real smile. A *strong* smile. A fluffy whipped-cream smile. I don't care that my teeth are natural, not a white-washed version of teeth. Not a row of Tic-Tacs. Turning in my cheap shoes, I march out and head for the elevator, knowing I can never turn back again. I'm on my way. Nobody can stop me now.

EIGHTEEN

I need a plan. The time has come to let everyone at *Scene* magazine know that Susanna Barringer has what it takes. It's not enough to stand up for myself, I have to *make* something of myself, too.

Yesterday, Nell asked me to walk her dog. She pulled a white fluff-ball out from under her desk and said, 'She prefers the hydrants on Lexington.'

Yes, I definitely need a plan.

In a bathroom stall, I call Amelia to set up a brainstorming session.

'How's Edgar?' I ask first.

'As crazy as ever. He wants to know if you're still looking up Nell's nose.'

I laugh. 'That's why I'm calling. Can you meet me for lunch?' I ask.

'My break is at one-thirty.'

'Brilliant!' I say, imitating Nell. 'Our usual spot?'

'Crikey!'

I laugh. 'I think crikey is *Australian*, Mel,' I say. 'And I think it means, "Yikes"!'

'Yikes!' she says, giggling.

We meet (sort of) halfway between Midtown and Uptown: the Central Park carousel.

I enter the park on East Sixty-Fifth Street. As I fast-walk past the zoo, I hear children squeal, and smell hay and sweaty animals. It's blistering hot out, but the grass is green and the old trees reach their branches out to shade me. This path into the park is one of my favourites. Elderly men play chess at stone tables, nannies push their babies in covered strollers, shirtless guys toss frisbees at one another. It's a postcard.

Mel waits for me at the carousel's entrance. Her pink hospital smock clashes with the white and red brick stripes of the big round building. Though I'm starving, and a hot-dog cart is right there, there's no line for the carousel and I can't resist taking a ride. It's only ninety cents – the best bargain in New York.

'Hop on!' I say to Mel, paying for her ride, too. We pick two horses next to one another. They are almost life-size. Creamy-white carved horses with chestnut manes and bright-orange saddles. My horse's head is lifted high, his mouth open. Amelia's fully-decorated stallion rears his head up as well, though his ears are pressed back. The music starts and off we go.

'What's up?' Mel asks me, as our horses rise.

'I need your help in devising a plan,' I say over the music.

'Ooh!' Mel's eyes light up and she reaches one hand into her handbag for a pad and pen. Which is so *her.* Even on a carousel, hanging onto the pole, Amelia would never dream of devising a plan without taking notes.

'Category?' she asks me, her pad perched on the saddle.

'Future career.'

'Problem?'

'Non-existent.'

'Ah. Nell's pores again?'

'Worse. Nell called me into her office to kill a cockroach the other day. A *huge* one. He ran into her bathroom and I had to run in after it.'

'Did you get it?'

'Yes. But he was swimming in the toilet before I flushed him down. He could have swam up by now.'

'Swum.'

I roll my eyes. 'The point is,' I say, 'if I don't do something quickly, the only thing I'll learn from my summer internship is that the British definition of intern is: don't even *think* you're not a servant.'

Amelia rides her horse up as mine floats down.

'Don't bite my head off, Susanna, but isn't that what interns are – servants?'

I sigh. 'I know I have to pay my dues, and I'm willing to do that. But, it's beginning to feel like I'm paying *rent.* If

I don't show Nell what I'm capable of doing before summer is over, she'll never know who I really am.'

'A wily New Yorker?'

'Exactly! Hence, the need for a plan.'

'Hence?'

'Yes, *hence*.'

'Got it.' I'm not sure, but I think Mel writes the word 'hence' on her pad.

'I work at *Scene* magazine, not some copy centre like Kinko's!' I continue.

Mel nods sympathetically.

I say, 'So, I'm thinking of moonlighting.'

'Moonlighting?'

'As a reporter for *Scene* magazine.'

We both laugh.

'Actually,' I say, 'I was thinking that, if I got a great story, you know, a *scoop* that the magazine wanted to publish, Nell couldn't help but take notice.'

'I'm liking it,' Mel says, jotting 'scoop' on her pad.

'But how? When I'm not searching for the perfect diet food, I'm delivering a manuscript or copying one. Unless two stars meet and fall in love in the break room or the bus-stop, a great story isn't going to drop in my lap.'

'True.'

'Still, there has to be a way.'

'*Has* to be.'

'Where do celebrities hang out? How can I get one to talk

to me? Do I just wander the city streets after work, hoping to spot someone strolling down Madison Avenue? Even if I did, what would I say? What would get Nell Wickham's attention?'

The music winds down and the horses slow. Amelia accidentally drops her pad. I hop off my horse to get it for her, and I suddenly stop.

'Hey, wait a minute!'

'What?'

'I've got it!'

'Tell me,' she says as she swings one leg off her horse.

'The perfect plan!'

'I'm all ears,' Mel says, retrieving her pad, again ready to write it all down.

Instead, I throw my arms around my best friend and say, 'You're awesome. Thank you *so* much!'

'What did I do?'

'You've given me the idea that will jump-start my future career.'

'Wow. Do tell.'

With the carousel stopped, I kiss Mel's cheek, then leap off the platform. 'No time to tell you now. Summer is ticking away.'

The last thing I hear as I run back towards the zoo is Mel shouting, 'Lunch was great, Susanna! We ought to do it more often!'

NINETEEN

I swallow hard as I step off the elevator at *Scene*. I'm sweating (of course) and blushing already. Still, I walk straight for the art department, my recently resprouted shoulders on a hanger. Now that I've decided Keith Franklin is essential to revving up my girl power and getting noticed by Nell, I know I must go where no measly intern has the right to go.

'Keith?' With nerve blotches bright red on my neck, I march into Keith Franklin's office with a notepad and pen in my shaky, sweaty hands.

'Susan, right?'

The nerve blotches slowly creep up my chin.

'Susanna, actually. I work with Nell.'

'Ah, yes. Nell's summer toady.'

I'm not sure what a 'toady' is, but I giggle girlishly because – well, can you *not* giggle girlishly when you're a *veh*-gin who's three feet away from such a visible tan line?

'What can I do for you, Susanna?'

I stop twittering and hold up my notepad. Mentally, I will my hand to stop shaking.

'I'm doing a report for school. Extra credit. For next year. And I was wondering, if it wouldn't be too much trouble, can I interview you?'

I hold my breath. Freeze in place. The notepad quivers midair.

'Sure,' Keith Franklin says, breezily, as a strand of his wavy, black hair tumbles out of his bandana and falls into the hollow of his amazing cheek. 'What about?'

I'm ready. I rehearsed this part on the way back from non-lunch with Mel.

'It's a report about different jobs. What people's day-to-day working lives are like. And you, being the staff photographer for *Scene,* would be in the *cool* job section.'

Keith chuckles. I plough on through my speech.

'It'll only take a few minutes. What I need to know is stuff like—' I gulp. 'Where do you actually *find* the celebrities you photograph for the "Seen" column of *Scene*? Do you wander the streets hoping to spot someone strolling down Madison Avenue? Or, are there *specific* places in the city where stars hang out? You know, that kind of thing.'

It's not easy lying to such a beautiful face, especially when I believe in karma. But, the way I justify it is this: isn't a lie really in the eye of the beholder? Isn't the line between lying and creatively advancing your future career too blurry to define? I decide that it is and command my face to stop looking so guilty.

Keith abruptly stands. 'Come with me,' he says, as he saunters past me in his low-riders, and makes a beeline for Nell's solar flare of an office.

I panic.

'It's okay, Keith, you don't have to do it. I was just asking. I'll get someone else,' I babble, but he doesn't turn around. The red blotches have now sprouted all over my face. Keith Franklin glides down the hall as I run after him. He marches straight through Nell's open door while I cower outside it, bracing myself to be fired from my non-paying summer toady job. How humiliating is that?

'Nell?' Keith asks.

'Yes, darling?'

'Can I borrow Susanna tomorrow?'

'*My* Anna?'

'Yes, I need a teen to act as decoy.'

'Fine.'

'Cool.'

'Ta-ta.'

'Later.'

Keith emerges from Nell's office and winks. I try to shut my gaping jaw, but it keeps plopping back open.

He says, 'Tomorrow you get the Keith Franklin personal celebrity tour. By the end of the day, you'll know exactly what I do for a living, and where I spot every star in New York. Good enough?'

My jaw still won't stay closed. Is this my karmic return

for hanging out with Edgar or joining my mom and The Trips in Hudson River Park?

Before Keith disappears into the art department, he turns to me and yells, 'Wear comfortable shoes. We'll be walking all day.'

TWENTY

I look it up the moment I get home.

Toad'y (to'de): n. sycophant.

Next, I look up 'sycophant'.

Syc'o'phant (sik'fant): n. self-seeking, servile flatterer.

That sounds about right. The other day, Nell flipped her blonde hair back and stroked her neck. 'Tell me honestly, Sue, do you think Vince Vaughn would ever ask me out?'

Honestly? No. Considering she's old enough to be his mom. And super-honestly, is she in *high school*? What, she wants Vince to carry her books or ask her to the prom? As Nell checked out her face in the mirror on her desk, I bit the inside of my lip to keep from smirking.

'Sure,' I said. 'Why not?'

Ever the servile flatterer.

Self-seeking? Well, I'm nothing if not a girl forever finding herself. So, I guess Keith Franklin had it right when he called me Nell's *toady*. Not that it matters. I'd follow him around Manhattan even if he called me a *toad*.

My big dilemma now, of course, is what to wear.

I'm not foolish enough to think Keith Franklin would ever

ask me out, but, admittedly, I *am* foolish enough to want him to want to – even though I *am* underage and unable to fit into the fashion closet clothes. Hey, a servile flatterer can have her fantasies, can't she? The important thing is *not* to look like Keith's kid sister. Especially when we'll be spending the whole day together.

My heart lurches. The whole day? On the streets? In the heat? With a guy who makes me sweat in air-conditioning? Constructing the ideal outfit will be the most challenging thing I've encountered so far this summer. Inspired by my best friend Amelia, I make a checklist.

SOPHISTICATED SWEAT-FREE OUTFIT

✓ White shirt, loose. (Make that ironed white shirt, tied at the waist.)
✓ Linen Capri pants. (Ironed, too. Definitely.)
✓ Check back view in full-length mirror. No visible panty line!
✓ Sandals? (Too risky. Sweaty feet and blister possibility.) White leather Keds? Yes. Especially since they are the only sneakers I have, unless you count the grungy tennis shoes I wear when I take The Trips to Battery Park.
✓ Thick anklet socks for comfort.
✓ Low ponytail. Classic. Cool. (No claw clips!)
✓ Waterproof mascara.
✓ Handbag, instead of backpack (less high schoolish). Fill with Kleenex, lipgloss, Listerine PocketPak, full MetroCard, cab fare

(just in case), sunscreen, and small, travel-sized talc for nooks and crannies.

✓ Notepad! Pen!

I'm ready. I call Mel and tell her what's going on.

'Fab!' she says. (Her Brit-speak is improving.)

While we're on the phone, Mel Googles Keith Franklin and announces, 'He's a Boy Wonder, you know. It says here that he's the hottest, youngest celebrity-photographer in publishing.'

My heart lurches again. Amelia doesn't have to tell me Keith Franklin is a Boy Wonder. One look into his turquoise-blue eyes is enough.

We meet at the south-east entrance to Central Park, beneath the gold-leafed and pigeon-pooped statue of General Sherman. Keith is sipping a tiny cup of coffee and ripping into a bagel with his white teeth. As I approach, I feel my armpits dampen. He wears a navy blue bandana today, and a tight, black T-shirt tucked into his jeans. The strap of his large camera bag perfectly bisects his buffed-up chest.

'Here.' He thrusts a paper bag in my direction. 'Hope you like sesame.'

I peer into the bag, see a sesame bagel and smell hot, strong coffee.

'I wasn't sure if you drink espresso yet,' he says, grinning a casual, lopsided grin, 'but I took a chance.'

'Of course I drink espresso,' I say. Of course, I *don't*. Not even regular coffee, unless it's beige with cream and so sugar-filled it could induce diabetes. Reaching into the bag, I pull out the espresso, take a sip, and try not to wince when the bitter, black coffee slides down my throat.

'Mmmm,' I say, trying to sound mature. Hadn't I heard my mother moan over the supposedly delicious taste of coffee every morning?

'So,' Keith says, a half-chewed bagel bulging out from his smooth, brown cheek, 'what do you want to know?'

What *do* I want to know? I gulp. Actually, I'm dying to know what his lips taste like. Cherries? Espresso? Will I be able to feel his moustache stubble when we kiss?

'Uh,' I say, as reality slaps me in the face and I realise I should have spent a moment or two thinking about the fake report I'm fake-writing. At least enough so I wouldn't now look like a politician when the teleprompter breaks down. My armpits are suddenly drenched. Thank God I'm wearing white.

'Maybe you just want to follow me around and take notes?' he asks.

'That would be good,' I say, exhaling. Trying to look relaxed, I take another sip. Does anyone actually *like* espresso? Are they the same people who like Brussels sprouts?

Keith takes a small step closer to me and says, 'There's only one rule, Susanna. Lay *low*. The secret to being a good celebrity-spotter and photographer is blending into the crowd.'

Yeah, like *he* blends into a crowd. A crowd of male models, maybe. Come to think of it, Keith looks more like Halle Berry than Nell does.

'Aren't you going to write that down?' Keith asks.

'Oh!' I nearly spill my espresso and drop my sesame bagel fishing around in purse for my notepad and pen.

Keith just laughs. 'I'm teasing you,' he says. 'Relax. We have a long day ahead of us.'

Pen and paper in hand, espresso and bagel in bag, I jot down the first note that will help me create my future career. *Relax*. Then I add *Lay low*, and underline it twice.

'Follow me, Susanna,' Keith says. 'First stop: the Plaza Hotel.'

TWENTY-ONE

Each time I push through the polished revolving doors into the lobby of the Plaza Hotel, I'm awestruck anew. The Plaza is *transporting.* It instantly takes you back to a time when women wore fussy hats over major hairdos, and men went insane at the sight of an ankle. The crimson carpet, alive with swirls of forest-green and magenta roses, cushions every step. A humungous crystal chandelier sparkles overhead. The soaring white ceiling is rimmed in gold. Elegant tapestries hang high on the walls. Giant bouquets of fresh flowers are everywhere. It smells sweet. Gentle waves of live harp music float through the air.

'Walk like you belong here.' Keith's pace is so fast it's hard to keep up.

I've dreamed of belonging here. Spending a long, luxurious weekend in a soft white bathrobe, on a bed that feels like a gigantic marshmallow, with a remote in one hand and a room-service menu in the other. Far from the Three Stooges and juice boxes and smelly baby wipes.

The renovation is awesome. Thankfully, they kept the

classy feeling of the old hotel when they created the new section of condos.

'Hotels go in and out of style,' Keith says quietly to me. 'The Plaza is hot again. That's a big part of my job – always knowing which restaurants and hotels cause a buzz.'

Keith turns left and marches past the gourmet chocolate shop, gift shop and restrooms that say 'Gentlemen' and 'Ladies'. He makes a sharp left and stops at a bank of four pay-phones.

'Ta-da,' he says.

I look around, see nothing.

'This is one of the best places to star-gaze in New York.'

Keith seems to enjoy my confused expression. He points. 'See those elevators over there?'

I nod.

'They are the *back* elevators. The front elevators, next to one of the hotel entrances, is where the front desk is. True celebs never check in at the front desk. The hotel manager escorts them into the hotel *here*.'

He points to a side door that says 'Emergency Exit Only'. It's next to a winding carpeted staircase that's closed off by a velvet rope.

'If they want total privacy, they walk up these stairs. If they can handle possibly running into a mere mortal, they take these elevators. Hardly anyone knows about these back elevators. Which is how the hotel likes it.'

My jaw drops.

'Often, I stand here pretending to talk on the phone. Eventually, a VIP will walk down the stairs, or come out of that elevator. When they do, I snap their picture.'

'Don't they get mad?' I ask.

'Celebrities get mad when you stalk them, or pop out of their hedges. They get angry when annoying *paparazzi* wait outside nightclubs trying to try catch them stumbling drunk or looking bad. That's not me. I'm a *photographer.* And, stars *want* to be in the public eye. Publicity propels their careers. Most of the time, they know I'm going to be looking for them and they're ready. They're looking for me, too.'

'Really?'

'Really. You'll notice that a star who hasn't had any press lately will show up at an event in an outrageous dress or on a loud Harley. They can't take being ignored for very long. It's all a game. The more successful you are, the better you play it.'

I write *Plaza Hotel phone bank*. Then, I add *Game*.

Keith takes off again and I scurry behind him. 'This way for the next stop on the Keith Franklin tour.'

Thank goodness I'm wearing sneakers.

Striding back through the front lobby and out the same revolving doors that led us in, Keith nods at the doorman, who is hailing a cab for a woman with a large pile of Gucci luggage. Quickly, I look at her face. But, she's nobody. Nobody I recognise, anyway. Just some rich woman who likes to announce her wealth each time she packs for a trip.

'Hurry up, Susanna.' Keith is flagging me from the bottom of the stairs. I quicken my pace, run with him past the circular fountain, to the corner of Fifth Avenue and Fifty-Eighth Street.

The traffic thins for a moment and Keith crosses against the red light. I leap into the street and follow.

'Where to next?'

He points. 'We're going to one of the biggest celebrity hangouts in the world,' Keith says, pointing. 'FAO Schwartz.'

When I was a kid, FAO Schwartz was one of the main reasons I liked being a kid. It's the most amazing toy store in the world. From the moment you step through the door, you're in fantasy land. It almost feels like being in Willy Wonka's chocolate factory, but instead of candy (though there *is* a candy shop upstairs!), there are toys everywhere. The first floor has the largest stuffed animals you've ever seen – even a life-sized stuffed elephant! Upstairs, there is a child-sized Mercedes, a piano you can dance on, and the most awesome dolls I've ever seen – including Barbies wearing real designer wedding dresses!

Unbelievably, this amazing store went bankrupt and closed for a while. But now, it's open and as awesome as ever.

'This is where stars buy toys for their kids,' Keith says.

Why didn't I think of that?

Keith briskly wanders through the aisles, glancing side-to-side. I follow him up the escalator, past the gargantuan flat-screen TV and enough action figures to stage a real battle on the streets of New York. Back down the escalator, he slithers through the stuffed bear section, and suddenly drops behind the thigh of a gigantic teddy. Yanking my arm, he pulls me down next to him.

'What's going o—?'

'Shhh,' he whispers.

In one fluid move, Keith whips out his camera, aims it, adjusts the telephoto lens, clicks twice, and tucks it back in his bag. I watch, stunned. There, near the cash register, is that woman who starred in that movie with that guy! I'm so thrilled, I forget her name. She's gorgeous. Her skin is like strawberry yogurt. Her long blonde hair is perfectly straight and trimmed. She's mega-thin. Much thinner than she looked when I saw her in that film wearing that amazing dress.

'Let's go,' Keith says. He stands and casually saunters toward the revolving exit door.

'You're *leaving*?' I ask, racing to catch up.

Outside, he says, 'Another secret to being a successful celebrity-photographer is to shoot and run. Just in case they do get annoyed; escape before they know you got them. And that –' he says, grinning '– was a good capture.'

'Capture? Like *America's Most Wanted*?'

'Exactly.'

Keith takes off and I scamper after him. The excitement of seeing a real, live star evaporates my nervousness around

Keith. I practically skip along beside him to the corner of Fifth Avenue and Fifty-Seventh Street. It's incredibly hot out, but, standing next to Keith Franklin, I feel almost cool.

'Celebrity Alley,' he says, with a sweep of his arms.

'This corner?'

'This whole street, from river to river. I hang out here a lot. You can always see someone.'

On my notepad, I quickly write a five and a seven and an exclamation point. Before I have the chance to write anything more, we turn right, toward the Hudson River, and we're off and nearly running again.

Keith was right when he said we'd be on the move all day. I'm *so* glad I didn't wear sandals! After patrolling 'Celebrity Alley' we circle back and continue our trek downtown.

'Celebs live on raw fish,' he announces. 'You can always catch someone at the hottest sushi restaurant in town.'

I write *Sushi*, and keep walking.

'Megu is good,' he says. 'And Nobu and Jewel Bako and Sushi Yasuda on the east side.'

Scribbling frantically, I hope I can read my own handwriting when I use this information to carve out a future career.

As he strides down Fifth Avenue, Keith peers into store windows with the pinpoint gaze of a professional celebrity-spotter. One squinty-eyed look in each store is all it takes. Keeping up with him – or trying to – has drenched my no-sweat outfit. So much for advance planning. But, I'm so grateful for the celebrity-sighter's blueprint, I don't even care that I look like a soggy dog.

'If you ever want to see stars, and you have time, hang out in the lobby bathroom of a hot hotel. Celebrities drink copious amounts of water. They think it's a fountain of youth. But really, it's just a constant stream of pee.'

Keith is full of tidbits like that. I can't write fast enough.

'Always look for the celebrity uniform.'

'Uniform?' I echo.

'Knit or baseball cap, sunglasses, baggy clothes.'

'Ah.' I scribble.

'And every successful photographer knows about the Mama Bear Syndrome. Never, under any circumstances, approach a star mom when she's with her kids. She'll tear your head off.'

We speed-walk downtown twenty blocks to Madison Square Park. By now, it's lunchtime, and I've nearly sweated myself to a size – uh, eight. We've been moving so fast I haven't had time to slip into a public restroom and talc my nooks and crannies! My feet sink into the asphalt each time we cross a street. My ankles are so swollen they look like dinner rolls. Perspiration drips down my face. Now I know why Keith wears a bandana!

I'm exhilarated. What an awesome day! We haven't seen a single celeb on the streets, but I now know where to spend all my free time this summer: back elevators, toy stores, hotel bathrooms and new raw fish restaurants!

Feeling brazen, I ask Keith, 'If you were a *reporter*, instead of a photographer, how would you get a celebrity to talk to you?'

Thankfully, he doesn't seem to question my motives. Quite simply, he says, 'Ask them a question they want to answer.'

Hmmm. Why didn't I think of that? Then, I think on it some more.

'What kind of question would a star want to answer?'

Keith laughs. 'Nothing anybody wants to read about, unfortunately. Which is why there's such a love-hate relationship between celebrities and the press. They crave publicity, we crave the story. They want it their way, we want it ours. The truly great reporters are the ones who can squeeze information out of a star without them even feeling it. But, reporters like that are hard to find.'

I nod and smile. I now know what I must do with the rest of my summer: not only find a great celebrity, but squeeze him so gently he won't even feel the pinch.

TWENTY-TWO

It's early afternoon. I've reapplied my sunscreen twice, though it keeps slipping off my sweaty face. I'm starving, but I'm not sure if lunch is included in the Keith Franklin tour. As if reading my mind, Keith stops next to a sidewalk vendor and asks me, 'Hot-dog or soft pretzel?'

Apparently, celebrity-photographers don't eat sushi at Megu.

'Pretzel,' I say, peering into the grey hot-dog water and making a face. I'm having a mega-carb day, but I'm also walking my butt off, so I figure I'm okay.

Keith buys two pretzels, hands me one, squirts brown mustard on his and tears into it the same way he tore into his bagel that morning. I tear into mine, too. I know it's not very dainty, but at this point, my fantasy of dazzling Keith Franklin with my maturity and hot looks is as limp as my sweat-drenched hair.

'How do you like working for Nell?' Keith asks me between bites.

I chew. I swallow.

'Fine. Great. I love it.' I lie.

He laughs. Clearly, he doesn't believe a word.

'You can't take anything she says or does personally,' he says. 'Nell treats everyone like a peasant.'

'I've noticed,' I say.

'I'm a peasant, too,' Keith says, 'if it's any consolation.'

It is. He grins at me, a wad of half-chewed pretzel in his cheek. Being a peasant isn't so bad, I think. At least you get to wear comfortable shoes and eat food that's cooked on the street.

'Look, Susanna, all you need to know about pleasing Nell is this: her entire world revolves around *Scene* magazine. With it, she's a star. She has *power.* Without it, she's just another Brit who secretly envies Americans because we broke away from Mother England and can now kick her royal ass. Nell will be happy with you if you help her keep her job. Period. That's all she really wants.'

I flash back to my third day on the job when Nell asked me, 'How old would you say I look?'

'I don't know,' I said, not sure if she wanted to look young or accomplished.

'Go on, take a stab.'

I took a stab.

'About fifty?' She looked older than my mom, younger than my grandmother.

Nell's face melted and she sank into the cushions of her white couch, as if I *had* stabbed her.

'Fifty is ancient in this business,' she muttered. 'I need another laser resurfacing.'

Keith leans close to me. 'Wanna know a secret?'

'Yeah.' I lean into him, too. I inhale and smell his fresh sweat, his shampoo. I feel the heat rising up from his brown skin.

'Nell was born in *Liverpool*.'

'Why is that a secret?'

'Her father was a crew member on the Mersey ferry. Her mom was a housewife.'

I blink twice. 'I don't get it,' I say.

Keith smirks. 'Nell is a peasant, too. She doesn't come from the upper class any more than you or I do. But Americans are so gullible, we believe that anyone with a British accent is automatically better and smarter than we are. We may act like bullies, but in our hearts, we're still the upstart kids who ran away from home – from England. No matter what we do, we'll always feel like kiddies next to big Mom and Dad.'

Willow. I'm tempted to visit her Sociology professor at NYU and demand he turn her A into an F. Clearly, she knows *nothing* about the real Nell Wickham.

Keith says, 'Nell is just like every other neurotic. She's terrified of being found out. She doesn't want anyone to know that she's just like everyone else.'

Nell, like everybody else? I imagine her running for a bus, with a Food Emporium bag in her hand and a hole in her drug-store stockings. Does Nell's sunscreen slide off her face?

I can't believe Keith Franklin told me Nell's secret. He's so unbelievably cool. Not at all like the hot boys at school who look at me like I'm the class clown, or their best bud. Keith has a sparkle in his eye. Like maybe, just maybe, he sees the *real* me. The pre-woman lurking inside my post-girl body, waiting for the right guy to kiss it awake. My heart flutters. Is it *possible* that Keith Franklin might one day look at me with *more* than a sparkle in his ey—

'Keith!'

Someone bumps me from behind. I see a blur of tan skin and blonde hair whoosh past me and fly into Keith's arms.

'Monique!' Keith says. '*Ça va?*'

Keith kisses the tallest, skinniest woman I've ever seen, on both of her perfectly jutting cheekbones. Clearly, Monique prefers the American version of 'hello'. She plants a long, lingering kiss right smack on Keith luscious lips. I stand there, staring, for what feels like my entire teenhood. When she's done, Monique pulls her lips back, but leaves her body pressed against Keith's. I notice that he doesn't seem to mind. He smiles and seductively says, 'You look hot.'

Earlier, when he said that to me, he added, 'Shall we rest in the shade for a few minutes?'

Quietly, I hide the remaining bites of my soft pretzel behind my back.

'I thought you were in Paris,' Keith says to Monique.

Monique answers with another kiss to Keith's lips. When she comes up for air, she says, 'I couldn't stand to be without you and American cigarettes.'

'In that order?' Keith asks.

'Mais non,' she answers in French.

Monique's thighs are the size of my upper arms. Next to her, I feel like a toad's toady. The wart on the chin of a toad's toady. The air itself seems to make me fatter and shorter. I can almost feel my cheeks getting round as I stare at the gorgeous hollows in hers. Monique would *never* eat a pretzel from a street vendor. Or, if she did, she'd take one bite and throw the rest away. I glance to the side, looking for a trash can.

'This is Nell's intern, Susanna,' Keith says, introducing me.

I reach out one hand – the one *without* the pretzel remains – but Monique bends down and kisses me on both cheeks. Her kisses make me feel dismissed. Voted off the island.

Keith says to her, 'I'm working now, but how 'bout drinks at Balthazar tonight?'

'I'll be waiting for you at the bar,' Monique says, pronouncing the 't' with a 'z'. At *ze* bar.

Monique twirls around and Keith and I both watch her walk away. Keith, with lust in his eyes. Me, with awe. How could this woman *not* be a model, with a body like that? Why would nature give her such broad shoulders and skinny hips if not to hang clothes perfectly on them?

'Where were we?' Keith asks.

The truth? I was in serious denial, imagining Keith Franklin would one day find me hot in the non-flushed-and-sweaty kind of way. Now, I'm in harsh reality. Back to being Nell's servile flatterer.

'I think we were wrapping up,' I say. 'I have everything I need. Thank you so much—'

'Ever watch the show, *Caught Off-Guard*?' Keith asks.

My heart goes *boing*!

'I *love* that show. Randall Sanders is in that show!'

Instantly, I forget all about Monique's cheekbones.

Keith smiles. Impossibly, he still looks as good as he did that morning.

'Follow me,' he says, shoving the last of his pretzel in his mouth. I follow, swallowing my fantasies along with the last bite of my pretzel.

We snake through foot traffic on Twenty-Third Street – over thirty blocks from the office! – smell the sweet aroma of the hot, sugared nuts sold from another corner cart. Keith turns right on Park Avenue South, and left on East Nineteenth. Ahead, on Irving Place, I see a row of square white trucks. Generators hum in the humid summer air, pumping air-conditioning into each trailer. Two uniformed police officers keep onlookers out by standing in front of a row of blue barricades. They chat and sip coffee from *Caught Off-Guard* mugs. Closer to the trailers, a guy in a tank top listens to voices on a walkie-talkie; another adjusts a huge floodlight so it shines directly into a parked car on the side of the street. Following the sound of a barking dog, I look up and notice that residents in the apartment buildings on either side of the street are pressed to their windows, watching.

My heart is now pushing its way out of my chest.

Keith ducks into a doorway and pulls me with him. He opens his camera bag and yanks out a small clipboard and a headset. 'Never leave home without them,' he says, removing his signature bandana, putting the headset on, and adjusting the microphone in front of his mouth. He tucks the long wire into the pocket of his jeans. It's not connected to anything, but nobody would know unless they pulled the wire out. He then rummages in his bag again and retrieves a fake photo ID that's suspended from a skinny chain. Putting it over his head, with the photo hanging down to his waist, Keith hands me the clipboard and says, 'Hold it close to your chest and lay low.'

Agog, I do as I'm told. Keith straightens up and whispers, 'Follow me, and walk like you belong here.'

Amazingly, Keith does exactly that. Pretending to talk into the headset, he marches around the barricades, waving at the police and holding up his fake ID. They wave back. Clipboard clutched to my pounding chest, I follow. Past the walkie-talkie guy, a real-live director's chair, and a huge camera on a rolling cart. Tons of people are standing around, but no one pays any attention to us. Keith, in character, reminds me to be careful as I step over the thick, black cables taped to the sidewalk. He waves at some phantom colleague in the distance, and nods to the real professionals standing around waiting for whatever is supposed to happen, to happen. The transformation is freakish. Keith is a totally different guy. He's now a television cameraman walking through a location shoot. He plays the part perfectly. Me, I'm too nervous to do anything but blindly follow him.

'Stand here,' Keith says, parking me next to a table full of food. He leaves to grab us a couple of fruit plates. Rows of bottled water are within my reach, and I'm dying of thirst, but I don't move. Instead, I force my face to look casual, reminding myself that I'm a wily New Yorker – yes, *wily* – and I can act every bit as confident as Keith does.

Then it happens.

First, I hear a woman's voice. It's incredibly nasal. And *loud.* She's across the street, where the trailers are, and her voice drowns out the generators, the walkie-talkie guy, and the dog who's *still* barking on the second floor of the apartment building behind her.

'We're ready,' she brays. 'Are you ready?'

The director nods. Everyone gets quiets. Even the dog shuts up.

Then *he* comes out.

From my position next to the food table, I see it all in slow motion. The trailer door opens with a long creak, a black boot steps onto the first of three stairs leading to the ground. A curly blond head tilts forward, brown velvet eyes look right, then left, then right at me. He smiles. I see the adorable chip in his front tooth and the sexy scar above his right eyebrow. He's short, but I can tell he's tall as a *person.* And, of course, he has the glow all stars have – celestial *radiance.*

I watch him fill his chest with humid city oxygen, purse his lips and blow the air out. Like a kiss. A steamy New York City kiss. At *me.* My heart does a samba. I feel dizzy. The clipboard slips from my fingers and hits the street with a *clack*! I open my mouth and lose my mind.

'Randall Sanders!' I shriek. 'Oh my God, it's Randall Sanders!'

So much for laying low.

TWENTY-THREE

The police are incredibly kind. They don't push or shove. They merely appear, one at each elbow, and gently guide me off the set.

'Was that me screaming?' I ask, mortified.

'Yes, hon, that was you.'

Trying to salvage a shred of dignity, I mutter, 'I dropped my clipboard.' Then, by way of a lame explanation, I add, 'I've been in love with Randall Sanders since I was ten years old.'

'That's nice.'

The police don't arrest me or anything. They do, however, escort me to the end of the block, to the other side of the barricades, and tell me that they *will* arrest me if I show up on the set again. Keith Franklin, I notice, is nowhere to be seen.

'Where do you live?' one of the officers asks.

'Horatio Street,' I mumble.

'Perfect timing,' the other officer says. 'Here comes the downtown bus.'

'But—'

Again, they don't shove me, but I do feel a tight squeeze on my arms as the bus door opens and I'm practically lifted onto the step. Before I have a chance to fish out my Metro-Card, the bus driver nods at one of the officers and waves me past the fare box. Apparently, perps don't have to pay.

'Thank you,' I say to the police, though I don't know why. They did just derail my fledgling career.

The bus door closes behind me and an officer taps it twice as if to say, 'Take her away. She's your problem now.' Red-faced, I stumble to the only open seat – at the rear. On my way to the back of the bus, I feel everyone's eyes on me in the sly way New Yorkers stare: beginning with your shoes, they take in every detail of your being – including manicure (or lack of one) and estimated price of haircut – without overtly looking at you at all. The New York brain is trained to process people instantly. Just the way everyone on this downtown bus is processing me right now. I *feel* them all calculating what crime I've just committed.

'Excuse me,' I murmur, as I squeeze into a two-seater nearly filled by a large man's double-wide butt. I never would have wedged into such an intimate seating situation had I not been feeling so humiliated. But, I'm too distraught to stand. All I want to do is burrow into the seat and stare at my white leather Keds (from Costco – which the passengers have already judged as lame).

How could I be so stupid? Yelling out Randall Sanders' name – *out loud*! How could my mouth work without a brain? Is there no end to the ways in which I can humiliate myself? Plus, Keith trusted me. How could I let him down when he'd spent the day helping me?

Sinking into the seat, I wonder, did I blow Keith's cover? Was he escorted off the set, too? Will Randall Sanders refuse to talk to *Scene* magazine again? Will Keith get in trouble? Will I be *fired*?

My mouth is so dry I gag each time I try to swallow. The large man next to me smells like my neighbourhood on a really sweltering day. But I'm not sure it's actually *him*. It could be me. And, the cops made me get on the wrong bus. I'm veering east when I should be veering west and I just passed Fourteenth Street where I should have gotten off and transferred to the cross-town.

My confidence is a limp tea bag. I can't move. It's entirely possible I'm wedged in this seat for life.

When my seatmate finally gets off the bus, I do, too. Outside, the muggy city air reminds me what an idiot I am. How could a day that started so right end up so wrong? How could my master career plan dissolve in one insane shriek?

Depressed, and afraid that I've hurt Keith's career too, I realise there's only one way I can deal with this right now. The 'hot now' sign is lit in the Krispy Kreme donut window up ahead.

TWENTY-FOUR

'Susanna? Is that you?' Dad whispers as I walk through the front door. I hear the warning in his voice: make noise and you're toast.

It's nap time. The Trips are asleep and my father is sprawled on the couch, staring vacantly at the ceiling. His flex-time arrangement at the lab means he's home in the afternoon three days a week while my mom is at work. By the look of our apartment, it has been a madhouse. Toys are strewn everywhere, cereal bowls are still on the kitchen table, an orange blob of food is stuck in my dad's hair.

'Tough day?' I ask.

'You could say that,' Dad says, wearily. 'You, too?'

I sigh. 'Your daughter is a moron,' I say.

Dad smiles, moves a leg to make room for me on the sofa and asks, 'What happened?' Then he adds, 'Don't tell me too loudly.'

Plopping down next to my dad, I softly tell him about Nell, my master plan for emancipation, and my meltdown the moment I saw Randall Sanders' gorgeous face.

He looks hopeful. 'Are you ready to return to your original plan of becoming a marine biologist?'

I groan. 'That was *fifth* grade, Dad. After our trip to the Baltimore Aquarium. Even Mom wanted to be a marine biologist after that trip.'

'It's not too late for your mother, either.'

I smile. 'You're just going to have to accept the fact that your only daughter is a shallow celebrity fiend.'

My father sighs. He smells of diaper-rash cream.

'How 'bout I consider you a budding scientist of *popular culture*?'

'Sweet!'

Then, my shoulders sag. 'Basically,' I say, dejectedly, 'I killed a career that hadn't even started. So much for master plans.'

Dad looks me straight in the eye and asks, 'So, what's your Plan B?'

'*Plan B?*'

'Who succeeds on the first try? Look at Christopher Columbus. He was attempting to sail to Asia and he ended up discovering America.'

Actually, I want to say, Columbus didn't 'discover' any place. He brought smallpox and malaria to the Native Americans already living here. But, I decide against it because my father and I have had this discussion before and he always mentions that the natives gave us syphilis. Not that it was their fault.

'Or Spence Silver,' Dad continues.

'Who?'

'Spence Silver set out to create the world's strongest glue and ended up inventing the *worst* glue. The only thing he could use it for was a little billion-dollar invention called Post-It Notes. And then there's little Frankie Epperson, eleven years old, who made the mistake of leaving a stirring stick in a bucket of soda pop outside in the freezing cold. His blunder created the popsicle!'

That's what I get for talking to a *real* scientist. My dad knows everything.

'Everybody needs a Plan B, sweetheart,' Dad says softly. 'If Spence Silver had given up when he made a mistake, what would we all stick around the front of our computers?'

I smile. If not for Spence Silver, what would Nell stick on the tower of Xeroxing I have on my table every day? As I reach up to kiss my dad on the cheek, a car alarm goes off outside on the street. We both freeze. It's one of those alarms that chirp and honk *and* blare a siren. Inside the apartment, there's silence for a moment. Then, we hear it. Henry starts crying first. I can tell it's him because Henry's wail starts low in his throat, then travels up the musical scale until it nearly shatters glass. Evan joins his brother with a hiccuppy kind of cry, and Sam eventually just starts yelling.

Dad sighs. 'They're up,' he says.

'And they're paging us,' I add.

Dad hugs me. 'You okay?' he asks me.

'I will be.'

'Good,' he says, getting up from the couch. On his way to calm my brothers, he turns to me and says, 'Since you're home early, Susanna, could you run to Duane Reade and buy more Pampers?'

TWENTY-FIVE

Today is even hotter than yesterday, but I step off the elevator at *Scene* dressed completely in black. If I'm going to get canned, I might as well dress the part. I even consider wearing a veil.

My heart pounding, I make my way past the editorial cubicles to the art department. Please God, I whisper under my breath, don't let Keith Franklin be fired because of me. Let him not be mad at me. Let hi—

'Aaaaahhhhh!' A shrill, mocking scream greets my ears the moment I enter the art department. Keith, wearing a backwards baseball cap and authentic army fatigues, slaps the back of his hand against his forehead, rolls his eyes into his head and dramatically sinks to the ground.

'It's Randall Sanders!' he shrieks girlishly. 'Someone catch me before I faint!'

Everyone in the art department bursts into laughter at Keith's imitation of me. Except, of course, *moi.* I want to crawl into a hole and die of embarrassment. I wish I *had* worn a veil. Clearly, the whole magazine knows what a dork I was yesterday. Nell has probably already hired a new toady.

Maybe Amelia can get me a job at the hospital. *Do you need an extra blanket? Can I empty your bedpan?*

Keith picks himself off the floor and walks over to hug me.

'I'm only teasing you,' he says, playfully pinching my chin.

Only? I want to say. Why don't *you* try being a fifteen-year-old virgin who panic-sweats in air-conditioning and once barely made it to the bathroom to throw up before an oral report! And, by the way, I can't *believe* Keith Franklin has his arm around me.

'You did good, Susanna,' Keith says.

I make a face. 'Yeah, right.'

'Seriously. Because of you, I got several great shots and the magazine got an exclusive.'

'Really?'

Keith leads me over to a drafting table and shows me an enlarged photograph of Randall Sanders. His eyes are wide open and his mouth is grimacing. Is that what I thought was a *smile*? The man recently dubbed 'America's Hunk' appears petrified. I can barely look.

'And this,' Keith says, taking his arm off me and holding up another big colour photo, 'is why I get the big bucks.'

Now, I not only *look*, but I can't believe my eyes.

'Is that . . .' I swallow hard. 'Is that . . . *me*?'

Keith says, 'Of course it's you. Was anyone else carted off by the cops?'

I'm staring at a photograph of my butt, primarily, and the backs of two police officers as they escort it onto the (wrong!)

downtown bus. You can see my elbows, too, and the faint outline of the back of my head. Nobody would know it was me, unless they were intimately familiar with my rear end and, truthfully, *I* rarely even look at it.

The photograph isn't the most upsetting part of this particular moment. The *headline* is. In bold letters, pasted on top of the picture, the headline reads:

Randall Sanders' Stalker Nabbed by Police

'It's a joke, right?' I ask Keith. 'You're not going to print that, are you?'

'Of course we're going to print it,' Keith says. 'Nobody will know it's you. It's the perfect shot.'

'Perfect shot? It's a *lie*.'

Even as I say it, I know I sound naïve. Which I'm not. Not in this arena, anyway. I understand media exaggeration. I'm familiar with paparazzi tactics. I know photographers yell shocking things to get a rise out of celebrities. I've watched *Celebrities Uncensored*. But, I want to protest, that's *my* butt you're using to lie about my favourite actor. Nobody was stalking him! I was just holding a clipboard!

'Look,' Keith says, 'this is the way it's done, Susanna. Nobody gets hurt. The article is about celebrity stalkers in general, not you. It's just an anonymous photograph. No big deal.'

Then, he adds the clincher. 'Nell is thrilled.'

Nell. In all the hoo-hah, I'd forgotten to check-in with my boss. She'll think I'm late again today. Whirling around, I race-walk to the other end of the office where I expect to find Nell draped over her glass desk, whimpering, 'Tea . . . Tea . . . Where's my organic green tea?'

'Susanna!'

Nell flags me into her office. 'Have a seat, darling.'

Susanna? Darling? An interesting development. I sit.

'Keith told me how absolutely fabulous you were yesterday. Truly a team player. Brilliant! We may even put Randall on the cover.'

My mouth opens.

'Well . . . I . . . it was nothing, really.'

Suddenly, I think, So what if I participate in a lie? A *fib*, really. A publishing fib for the sake of news-stand sales. I *am* a team player. I'm even wearing the *Scene* uniform: black. My heart beats faster. What brilliant luck! My blunder made Nell call me *darling*! She even called me Susanna! My messenger/coffee-getter/dog-walker/cockroach-killer days are over! Who needs a Plan B when one little photograph of your (slightly large) rear propels you off the bench and into the game?

'Did you have a chance to swing by the florist this morning?' Nell asks.

'Florist?' I blink.

'Did I forget to tell you?' Nell shrugs. 'Silly me. I've decided I want fresh flowers every morning. Red tulips in spring, white Narcissus in winter, purpl—' She arches one of her freshly-plucked eyebrows. 'Shouldn't you be writing this down?'

'Uhhh.' My mouth has been hanging open so long I nearly drool. I'm a team player now! I don't get flowers!

'Oh, wait. What am I saying?' Nell twitters.

I exhale. Shut my mouth. *Whew*, that was close.

'Who cares what *type* of flowers they are as long as they're fresh! Just pick up whatever the florist thinks is best. In fact, run along and fetch me some right now, would you. I'm suddenly feeling a tad soggy.'

Fetch? I'm her *dog* now? What happened to my team?

Nell picks up the phone and instantly forgets I'm in the room. Feeling as though I've been slapped in the face, I rise and bite the insides of my cheeks to keep from crying. My eyes sting. I move fast, anxious to make it to the bathroom before tears erupt. Once inside a stall, I can continuously flush the toilet so no one hears me cry.

'Oh, Susan?' Nell cups her hand over the phone and catches me just before I'm completely out the door.

Turning, silent, I bite harder on my cheeks.

'Never lilacs, okay?' she says. 'I adore the colour, but despise the smell.'

TWENTY-SIX

Amelia calls me in tears. Edgar is getting worse.

'The doctors were in his room all morning. He's stable now, but he won't open his eyes. He can, but he doesn't want to.'

Instantly, my petty problems shrivel up. I ask, 'What can I do?'

Mel says, 'Come to the hospital after work. I know it's ridiculous to freak out over someone I knew wouldn't be here for ever. But I am, and I can't go through this without you.'

'I'll be there.'

One good thing about life and death – it keeps fetching Nell's flowers in perspective. Not to mention big butts on a bus, tiny clothes and humungous four-hundred dollar shoes.

After work, I call my mom to explain why I'll be late for dinner.

'Who? What? A *dying* man?' she asks, alarmed.

'It's okay, Mom. He's cool with it, and so am I.'

'What?'

I don't get it, either. All I know is, Mel needs me and I'm at the subway stairs.

'I'll be home as soon as I can,' I tell my mom before hanging up.

The train rumbles in shortly after I reach the platform. There's an open seat by the door. I can see my worried expression in the reflection of the facing window. What if Edgar is gone when I get there? Will I see something gross? How will I comfort my best friend?

'Chill out, Susanna,' I mumble under my breath. 'You can handle whatever happens. Be there for Mel.'

I keep telling myself that. Hoping it will be true.

As it had before, the hospital smells like a freshly-scrubbed floor. Somehow, though, the air *feels* different. Heavier, harder to move through.

I take the elevator up to Amelia's floor, walk past the nurses' station. My heart pounding, I make my way slowly down the hall, toward Edgar's room. You can handle whatever happens, I repeat. Just deal with it. For Mel.

It's quiet. Too quiet. I pass open doors, see family members holding the hands of their loved ones lying in bed. Someone is snoring. I feel my pulse shoot through the veins in my wrists.

Edgar's door is open a crack. A sliver of light spills into the hallway. My heart is now thumping so hard it hurts. I hear a noise. Two noises. It's not until I get right up to the door that I recognise what those noises are.

Mel and Edgar are *laughing.*

'. . . so she threw up her hands and said, "Why not marry the schmuck?"'

Relief floods my whole system as I push the door open and walk through.

'The mute!' Edgar cries.

Amelia runs and hugs me. 'Eddie came back,' she says, beaming.

'The human body is like the human spirit,' he says. 'Both are hard to kill.'

I barely know the guy, but I want to throw my arms around him and kiss him on his smiling lips. Machines blip all around his head. One arm is orange from the antiseptic they smeared on it. There's a new needle in his vein. Though Edgar certainly doesn't look *cured,* he's far from gone.

'Apparently, there's a waiting list for the hereafter,' he says, grinning.

A doctor pokes her head in the room and says, 'Two more minutes.'

We nod.

Edgar often reaches for his push-button – a zap of morphine, I find out, when the pain gets too great – but he seems even more lively than he was the last time I saw him.

'Mel tells me you want to devote your life to public service,' he says, winking at me. I wince.

'It's shallow, I know,' I say. 'Lately, I've been wondering if my dream of being a celebrity-reporter is really a nightmare.'

Edgar attempts to sit up. Mel helps him by propping a pillow under his back.

'Never be embarrassed by something you're passionate about,' he says. 'You're not hurting anyone. Besides, I love Hollywood, too. I'm a *huge* Randall Sanders fan.'

'You are?' I squeal.

'I can't believe they cancelled *Breach of Contract.*'

'I *loved* that show! Did you see his episode of *The Clock Ticks Backward*?'

'Hated the moustache.'

'The moustache was *hideous.* What was he thinking?'

'Are you going to see *The Man in the Window* when it comes out?'

'If I could stand up, I'd be first in line.'

Mel laughs. 'You two sound like Ebert and Roper.'

Edgar suddenly presses his eyes shut and squeezes the button in his hand. He doesn't open his eyes right away. Mel and I glance at each other.

'Next time, will you bring me an issue of your magazine?' Edgar asks me.

'Yes,' I say. 'In fact, I'm a real arse in next week's edition.'

I tell Edgar and my best friend everything, including how I now need a Plan B or I'll remain Nell's Lady-In-Waiting for *life.*

Mel tells me, as always, exactly what I need to hear.

'If anyone can get a great story, Susanna, it's you.'

'Think *Star Trek,*' Edgar adds.

'*Star Trek?*'

'Boldly go where no one has gone before.'

We laugh. The three of us are singing the high-pitched *Star Trek* theme when the doctor returns and joins in.

Edgar stops, closes his eyes and presses his morphine button again. The doctor nods at us and we know it's time.

'We've got to go,' Mel says softly, touching Edgar's arm.

Opening his eyes, he says, 'Go *boldly.*'

TWENTY-SEVEN

The great thing about New York City is the fact that you can't feel sorry for yourself very long because there's always someone who has it much worse than you. Like a homeless person, or Edgar, or the guy I see on the street this morning wearing a plywood placard on his front and back. It reads: 'Free soda with lunch special.' Shoulder straps keep his mini-billboards in place. They must weigh a ton. The air is so humid it feels like you're inhaling oatmeal. His face is purply-red and his hair hangs like tiny wet ropes beneath a baseball cap.

'Free soda with any lunch special,' he says, in case no one reads his sign.

Though a little ragged around the edges, he looks nice enough. He's in his early twenties. I check out his grungy sneakers and grubby fingernails and figure he went to state school in Queens. He didn't have a date for his senior prom – too shy. Now, he probably lives in Red Hook, Brooklyn, and plans to go to community college . . . someday.

'Lunch special and free soda,' he says, handing me a paper menu.

I take the menu, smile, and find myself grateful for the air-conditioning at *Scene* magazine. Even though I'm sweating now, and every time I have to messenger page proofs to agoraphobic writers, I know I'll eventually be back in the cool air around *Scene's* Xerox machine. It could be worse. Nell could ask me to stand in front of the building wearing a plywood enlargement of this week's cover. Yes, it could be much worse than picking up anything-but-lilacs every morning for the rest of the summer.

While I wait for the flowers (who charges two hundred bucks for a few flowers and some squiggly sticks?!) I think about my Plan B. Nell has flattened me, but she hasn't stomped out my spirit. There's still a glimmer of hope that I, Susanna Barringer, will come up with the magazine equivalent of a Post-It Note. I'll snag the story of the century. Stalking? That's *so* yesterday. My scoop on Randall Sanders will be as fresh as the flowers I'm now waiting to deliver.

I call Amelia on my cell to check on Edgar.

'He's hanging in,' she tells me. Her hushed tone lets me know she can't talk right now.

'I'll call you later,' I say before I hang up. Besides, Nell's flowers are ready.

Outside, the human billboard is still working in the heat. He tries to hand me another menu, but my arms are full of lilies – or are they irises?

'Keep it real,' he says to me.

'Thanks,' I reply, heading back to work. Then, I smile.

Keep it real. A guy I worked with last year on the yearbook staff used to say that every day.

'Keep it real, Barringer,' he'd mutter as we pored over candid campus shots. 'Keep it re—'

Suddenly, I stop dead on the sidewalk. The synapses in my brain fire all at once. It's Independence Day inside my head. Holy Nell! I've *got* it! My Plan B. All of a sudden, I know exactly how to get a great story on Randall Sanders. A *bold* story, an original! It's perfect! Why didn't I think of it sooner? I want to kiss the Menu Man to thank him for his inspiration. I want to hug Edgar for encouraging me to follow my passion. I want to thank the universe for giving me this idea. I even want to throw my arms around Nell Wickham for sending me out on the blistering streets of New York where brainstorms can unexpectedly materialise out of stinking, muggy air.

TWENTY-EIGHT

Nell loves the flowers; she simply *adores* them. She goes on and on until I'm quite sure I'll be standing there, in her office, listening to every floral adjective known to womankind, for the rest of my life.

'See how these silken petals are united in a perfect tubular corolla?'

I nod. I look at the tubular corolla, whatever *that* is, even though I really want to roll my eyes and check my watch. Nell may have all day to fawn over some flora, but I have serious work to do.

'I'll be at my des—' I start, taking a step toward the door.

'The yellow in this anther is the most delicious colour I've ever seen. Have you seen a more luscious hue, Suze?'

Now she's calling me *Suze*? I hate the name, Suze, even more than Susan.

Before I can answer, Nell is smearing yellow pollen on her eyelid and asking me, 'Does this accentuate the golden flecks in my eyes?'

Instantly, I wonder if I'm on a hidden camera. I mean, the woman just rubbed part of a flower on her face! Don't normal people try to keep pollen *away* from their eyes? Then, I remember who I work for.

'Yes, Nell. Your eyes look gorgeous. And young. You look like a model. Or an actress.'

'Brilliant!'

Nell rushes over to me, another pollen-tipped anther between her fingers, and rubs the yellow allergen into the back of my hand.

'Get over to Barney's or Sephora or Chanel and get me that colour!' she commands.

'Pardon me?' My nose begins to run.

'I want that exact colour in eye-shadow. It makes me feel, oh, I don't know, *randy.* I'm quite sure you'll find it somewhere in this city. You must! Perhaps the Body Shop or Origins? I don't care where you get it as long as it's an exact match.'

'But—'

'Is there a problem, Ann?'

Nell blinks haughtily. With her one yellow eyelid, and bright-red lips, she looks like a clown from Cirque du Soleil.

'No,' I lie, feeling a gigantic sneeze – and an even bigger headache – coming on. What, I'm her personal shopper now, too?

'Take all day if you need to. But, I simply must have that colour shadow by tonight. I'm going to a benefit for something endangered and I want to look a bit dangerous myself.'

Dumbfounded, I stand and stare.

Nell glares at me. 'What are you waiting for? Go! And bring me back a mango. A *ripe* one.'

I go. Before I can sneeze the pollen off my hand (and wonder if Mr Billboard has the ideal job after all), I walk over to my desk and tear off a piece of Scotch tape. Carefully sticking the tape directly over the yellow smear on my hand and pressing the top of it, I pull it up and transfer it onto a white piece of paper. Being the daughter of a forensics scientist – not to mention years of watching every version of *CSI* – have paid off. I now have a permanent 'fingerprint' of the colour I need to match. I can wash my hands. What I *don't* have, however, is any time to put my Plan B into action.

Or, do I?

The synapses in my brain start sparking again. Nell *did* tell me to take all day if I need to. It *is* barely nine o'clock. What if I find pollen-yellow eye-shadow by ten and use the rest of my 'looking' time to advance my future career? That isn't cheating, is it? I'll be working for *Scene* magazine one way or another, won't I? Nell will thank me!

Freshly inspired, I stash my 'pollen print' in my handbag, and dash over to the heart and soul of *Scene* magazine – the celebrity file room. Anyone who's anybody has at least *something* on file here. And Randall Sanders, well, he has an entire cabinet drawer filled with magazine clippings, reviews, photographs, interviews and – most importantly – personal information.

It takes me all of five seconds to find what I'm looking for. But I'll spend the rest of my life thanking the cosmos for giving me such good luck. The first stop on my way to getting that stellar story on Randall Sanders is only a train ride away.

TWENTY-NINE

Inspired – once again – by my best friend Mel, I make a list. I even devise a name for the adventure I'm about to embark upon. Since I'm determined to swallow my failures and Plan-B-it until I succeed, I call my journey 'Operation Spence Silver' after the Post-It Note guy.

Brilliant!

OPERATION SPENCE SILVER

1. Find Nell's mustard-coloured eye-shadow that makes her look like a jaundiced clown.
2. Call Amelia and see if she can leave work early – like NOW. Ask her if you can borrow ten bucks. Make that twenty.
3. Meet Amelia at Penn Station in half an hour.
4. Find New Jersey Transit ticket window.
5. Buy round-trip train ticket to Ridgewood, New Jersey.
6. If Amelia can't take the day off, beg her.
7. Don't tell parents you did this until it's over and Nell is so impressed with your creativity she'd rather die than ever again ask you to stop at every news-stand in Midtown to buy up all the

issues of 'New York' magazine with the unflattering profile in it calling her an 'Anna Wintour wannabe' before the real Anna Wintour sees it.

8. Go boldly.
9. Don't forget ripe mango!

THIRTY

'*Pleeeeeease!*'

As it turns out, I *do* have to beg. Mel is totally up for the adventure, but decidedly against asking any other volunteers to cover for her at the hospital because, well, that's the way she is.

'C'mon, Mel, *pleeeeeeease*,' I plead. 'It'll only take a couple of hours. Edgar is doing fine, isn't he? We'll have *fun*.'

'Eddie is having a good day, but I can't just *leave*,' she says. 'How responsible is that?'

'I'm not asking you to *walk out*. Can't you see if they don't need you for one tiny little afternoon?'

My best friend sighs. I move in for the kill.

'I *need* you, Mel,' I say softly. 'How can I continue to boldly go without you by my side?'

'You split the infinitive, Susanna.'

'Huh?'

'Never mind. Hang on for a second.'

Mel puts me on hold and I cross my fingers. While I wait, I remember English Grammar class and the split-infinitive rule that I always forget: never put a word in-between the root of a verb. As in the root being 'to go' and the splitter being 'boldly'. 'To go boldly', is okay. 'To boldly go' is not. Even though *Star Trek* got it wrong, trust Amelia to get it right.

'You still there?' she asks me, as she comes back to the phone.

'Where else would I be?' I say.

'In front of Penn Station in twenty minutes?'

I squeal. 'You're the best!'

'What can I say? I'm a sucker for adventure.'

'Operation Spence Silver here we come!'

'Who is Spence Silver?'

I laugh. 'Next to you, he's my role model.'

Before Mel hangs up and we both race to Penn Station, I ask one more thing. 'Can I borrow twenty bucks?'

Each time I descend the Seventh Avenue escalator into Penn Station, I feel both excited and sad. Sad, because I saw this show on PBS about the original Pennsylvania Station. It used to be two city blocks of pink granite, with a sky-high glass ceiling. Six humungous stone eagles guarded the entrance, and the floor inside was a checkerboard of marble and glass bricks. Now, it's essentially an underground mall with ticket windows in the basement, below Madison Square Garden. Most of the original building was torn down to make room for an office building and a sports arena! I mean, couldn't they find somewhere else to play basketball?

Still, I can't help feeling excited, too. Penn Station reeks of adventure! It reeks of popcorn and pizza – and the occasional homeless man who hasn't seen a shower or a toothbrush all summer too – but adventure is definitely in the air.

Since part of the original building is still standing across the street (it's a post office now), they say they're going to eventually move the mail carriers out and bring a beautiful train station back. I'm pretty sure they will, because the city fixed up Grand Central Station a few years ago – the train station on the east side – and it's awesome. There are lit-up constellations on the ceiling and everything.

'I feel like a spy on a secret mission,' Amelia says, as we join the stream of humanity.

In a way, that's exactly what we are.

Though it's after the morning rush hour, tons of people are still speeding through the corridors. Some roll suitcases behind them. Others carry briefcases. Cell phones are pressed up to a hundred ears.

'Look for signs that say "New Jersey Transit",' I say to Amelia.

We're both flushed, having raced across town and downtown to meet in the station. No way did I have time to buy Nell's eye-shadow yet, but I'm not freaking out. Macy's is a block away. I can shop for her when I get back from Jersey.

'There!' Mel points to a sign and we turn left to hop on another escalator. I look around and see all the people who work in Penn Station, day after day, *underground.* If they get up really early, and get home really late, they *never* see sunlight! How weird is that?

'Maybe they sunbathe all weekend,' Amelia suggests.

'Or maybe they're a mutant form of vampire,' I say.

We both shrug. The line leading to the New Jersey Transit ticket windows is straight ahead. We don't have time to speculate further.

Thankfully, the line is super-short.

'Two tickets on the next train to Ridgewood, New Jersey,' I say to the man on the other side of the Plexiglas window.

'Round trip?' he asks.

'Yes.'

A machine spits out four tickets that are about the same size as movie tickets. 'That'll be nine dollars and seventy-five cents each,' he says.

I look at Mel. 'Can I borrow that twenty bucks right now?' I ask.

She laughs, pulls a twenty out of her wallet and slides it beneath the glass. While the ticket-taker is making change, I study the schedule.

'There's a ten o'clock!' I say to Mel.

'If you hurry,' the ticket-taker says, 'you can catch the train on track twelve.' Pointing to the stairs on our left, he pushes Mel's change through the slot.

'Let's go!' I squeal, and off we run with Mel clutching her change in her fist.

Amelia and I dash down the long staircase. We feel rumbling beneath our feet. The train is just pulling in.

'Hurry,' I shout, even though Mel is racing down the stairs ahead of me.

On the red platform below, we see a train pulling in. Chests heaving, Mel and I reach the bottom of the stairs as train doors open with a *whoosh.*

'Main line to New Jersey! All aboard!'

I can't believe the conductor actually says 'all aboard' like in the movies.

Out of breath, but fizzing with the thrill of adventure, we leap on one of the cars and find two seats next to one another.

'We made it!' Mel says, hugging me. 'I'm so glad you begged me to come with you.'

'Me, too.'

Our seats are soft brown leather. The air smells of coffee. Almost instantly, the train pulls out of Penn Station and we're on our way. Leaning back, I take a deep breath and exhale. I listen to the *chuga-chug, chuga-chug* of the train and feel the gentle swaying from side to side.

'You're *my* role model, too,' Mel says, squeezing my arm.

Soon, we enter a dark tunnel under the Hudson River. Then, *poof*! The tunnel spits us out into daylight and we're in New Jersey. Just like that. I stare out the window at passing warehouses and fields of weeds. Ahead, I see the Secaucus station.

'This is where we get off,' I say.

'Already?' Mel asks.

'Follow me.'

We step off the train, ride an escalator up, walk over to another escalator, take it down, walk around, and descend again to another platform to catch a transfer train on the Bergen County line. Since transfer trains run so frequently, one arrives within five minutes. All told, it takes about an hour to get to the town of Ridgewood. As soon as we're settled into the rhythm of the train ride, we're there.

'Voilà!' I say to Mel.

Together, we step off the train; Part Two of our adventure begins.

So far, it's one of those semi-perfect days. I say 'semi' because my butt *was* photographed by Keith Franklin (which means he actually had to *focus* on it) and Nell *did* treat me like a dog named Sue. But, once Amelia and I get off the train at Ridgewood Station, Operation Spence Silver goes like clockwork.

'It feels like we're cutting class,' Amelia says, giggling.

We hurry for the main drag. Ridgewood is full of pretty stores with cutesy names like: Bagelicious, Jekyll and Hide Leather Goods, and a pharmacy they call an Apothecary.

'I can't believe Randall Sanders grew up here,' I say. 'It's like Disney World. It's so . . . so . . . *quaint*.'

As we power-walk, the town gets even quainter.

'I don't think "quainter" is a word,' Mel says, when I share my observation with her.

'It is now,' I say. And, why not? Was *bling* a word before someone made it up?

Together, Mel and I hurry past a Gap, a Baby Gap, a Starbucks, a bookstore called Bookends, and a Häagen Dazs ice-cream shop, before it occurs to me I have no idea if we're headed in the right direction or not.

'Is Ridgewood High nearby?' I ask a woman parking her SUV.

'Yes,' she says, pointing. 'Straight ahead. You can't miss it.'

My heart thudding, I walk straight ahead, knowing my future career is just up this beautiful, sunny street.

Mel and I walk . . . and we *walk.* Past a funeral home that looks like a Mexican hacienda, an animal hospital that looks like a Holiday Inn, and a Baptist church that looks like a neat pile of rocks.

'You sure we didn't pass it?' Mel asks, voicing my worry, too.

'She said we couldn't miss it,' I say. Then I check my watch. It's now eleven-thirty. 'We'd better walk faster.'

Huffing and puffing, we step up the pace. I feel my nose getting sunburned and my shirt getting sweat-stained. Still, I chug forward. Suddenly, rising up like a brick castle, we see a gorgeous fortress ahead.

'That can't be it,' I say. 'No way is that a high school.'

My school, though one of the best state schools in the city, looks like a prison. Metal-meshed windows and all.

Amelia and I cross the street and march closer to the 'castle'. A bright-red running track surrounds the bright-green grass of a soccer field. Peaked roofs rise up from the maroon brick. There's even a moat! A trickling stream runs along the front of the beautiful building.

'This has to be it,' Mel says.

'Man!' I say. 'Randall Sanders went *here*!'

Mel and I, both born in New York City, stare at the high school as if it were a mirage. You can't hear a single horn honking or a nutcase shouting about the size of alien pupils.

'Let's hurry,' I say, bringing us both back to the task at hand.

The front door to the school is unlocked (another huge difference from my school) and we walk right in. There aren't even any metal detectors! Since summer school is in session, we blend in easily. But, there aren't many kids hanging around the halls at all. The few who are – well, let me just say they *wouldn't* get hired to be Nell Wickham's ordinary teen summer toady. These students have 'ivy-league' written all over them.

'Can you point me in the direction of the library?' I ask a girl with shiny blonde hair and skin that wouldn't need *any* digital retouching.

'Sure.' She points down the hall, and I notice she has a professional manicure. Don't ask me how I can tell. I just can.

'Walk up the stairs, around the corner, and there it is,' she says.

'Thanks,' I reply, turning to leave. Amelia doesn't budge.

Mel says to the girl, 'I'm curious about something. Have you already decided on a career?'

The girl laughs. 'Of course I have. I plan to be the first female President of the United States.'

'Of course,' Mel says, dryly.

'Unless Hillary beats me to it.'

'Thanks for the directions to the library,' I say, tugging Amelia's sleeve. 'We've got to go.'

The moment we're out of earshot, I ask Mel, 'What was that about?'

'Just testing my theory: blondes in summer school are delusional.'

I laugh. 'How come I've never heard this theory before?'

'I just formulated it.'

We're both chuckling up the stairs and around the corner. But, the moment we get to the library, we're stunned into utter silence.

'*Closed?*'

'Closed?' Mel repeats.

'How could a school library be closed during summer school?'

We both stand there, staring through the window into darkness. I try, but I can't move. Disappointment has glued my feet to the floor.

'What do we do now?' Amelia asks me.

I have nothing to say to her. How many times can my

career end before it's begun? I feel like curling up in front of the locked library door and waiting until fall. I feel like—

'Hey,' I say, suddenly. 'What about a *public* library? It might be open!'

'Let's do it!' Mel says.

With renewed energy, we race to the front door. Operation Spence Silver is back on track. Outside, we ask another student where the town library is, and he points us in the right direction. Admittedly, I am beginning to feel a bit panicked. It's now nearing lunchtime. I hear the *tick*, *tick*, *tick* of Nell's impatience in my head. Is she wondering where I am? Or, more likely, where her *eye-shadow* is? Is she peckish? *Sue! Susan! Suzanne! Susie! Suze!* Has she exhausted herself screaming out my names?

Together, Mel and I run all the way to the library. By the time we get there, we're both sweaty and gasping for air. But, I have no time to lose. I drag myself to the reference desk and ask the librarian, 'Do you – *gasp* – have the – *gasp* – 1994 yearbook – *gasp* – for Ridgewood High?'

'Looking for Randall Sanders?' she asks. Her arms, in a grey cardigan sweater (in summer!) are crossed in front of her chest.

My mouth, already gaping open, gapes even more.

'Surely you don't think you're the only girls to come in here looking for Randall Sanders' high-school yearbook?' she asks.

Well, um, *yeah,* we had.

'I'm not looking for his photo,' I say, inhaling deeply, desperate to catch my breath.

'You're not?'

'No, we're not.'

She looks suspicious. 'What *are* you looking for?'

I take a deep breath. Try to calm myself. Boldly go.

'I need to know who Randall Sanders took to his prom.'

THIRTY-ONE

It's the obvious question.

'Why are you trying to find Randall Sanders' prom date?' the librarian asks.

My first impulse is to remain, um, *undercover* and make up some story like this: 'She's probably my birth mother. I found adoption papers in my parents' safe after they were killed in a fiery plane crash, and it listed the name of someone who went to Ridgewood High and dated Randall—'

On second thoughts, I realise Mel is standing right next to me. She'll probably burst out laughing. Plus, my best friend hasn't quite come around to my way of thinking, namely, that being 'undercover' isn't actually lying. Amelia can be so literal.

'Do you know her name?' The librarian fills the silence with another annoying question.

Now, I'm tempted to ask her, 'Isn't this a *public* library? Are you allowed to ask so many *private* questions?'

Suddenly, it feels like the whole world is staring at me in my sweaty sports bra and another pair of ripped flowered pants. Even Mel is gawking with her mouth open. Cracking under the pressure, I blurt out, 'Pretty soon, Nell will have me giving her pedicures! I hate other people's feet!'

Like fire from a dragon's mouth, the truth comes spewing out.

'Do you have any idea how hard it is to find sugarless, wholegrain scones?' I wail. 'If I don't turn things around fast, I'll never be emancipated!'

The librarian laughs. 'Come with me,' she says.

Mel and I follow her into a room filled with private reference books.

'Sit down.' She points to a small table. We sit. She disappears. Two minutes later, she hands me a maroon-coloured yearbook and says, 'Good luck.' Then, she leaves us alone to (hopefully) get what we came for.

The yearbook falls right open to Randall Sanders' senior photo. Clearly, the librarian was right; we weren't the first to check out our favourite star in his high-school habitat. The page is dog-eared and smudged. There's even a faint lipstick mark in the margin near Randall's photo.

'His hair looks geeky,' Mel observes.

Darker than it is today, Randall Sanders had messy, grunge hair. He also had a goatee that looks like a smear of chocolate pudding. The tiny chip in his front tooth that I find so irresistible isn't there. I don't see the delicious fingernail clip of a scar over his forehead, either. (Must have gotten them while doing his own stunts. That's *so* like him.)

Plus, he was called 'Randy' then. Which makes me think of Nell and her putrid yellow eye-shadow.

'We'd better speed it up,' I say, remembering how much more we still have to do.

The prom shots are in full colour right in the front of the yearbook. And there, of course, is *Randy.* Even with a lame goatee, he's hot. And popular. He's in two candid shots. In one, he's sticking his tongue out. In another, he's romantically knotted up with some blonde on the dance floor.

'That must be her,' I say. Mel nods.

'Tina Weikert,' she says, reading the caption.

Admittedly, I'm a tad disappointed. I was hoping Randall Sanders' prom date would look a bit more like – well, *me.* Instead, she looks like every other popular high-school girl who snags a guy like Randy Sanders. She has blonde hair (of course) which is straight (of course) and long (of course). She's tanned and I don't see a single freckle.

'Looks like she's a vegetarian,' Mel says. I agree. Who else could be so naturally thin? Plus, even though her eyes are closed, I can tell they are blue. Baby-blue. I can just *tell.*

After finding her in other candid shots throughout the yearbook, I notice that Tina Weikert doesn't look bad in a single one. Unlike a certain someone who was captured for *eternity* in a middle-school yearbook over-laughing at some stupid joke and looking like Seabiscuit, with gargantuan horse-teeth.

In all honesty, Tina Weikert looks nice. The kind of girl who has it all, but doesn't treat you like a skank for barely having any.

'What do we do now?' Mel asks.

I close the yearbook with a loud *whomp.*

'We find her,' I say.

THIRTY-TWO

With Mel on one computer and me on another, we both log online. The librarian lets us use the computers even though we don't have New Jersey library cards.

'But there's a fifteen-minute time limit,' she warns.

'That's fine,' I reply, looking at the wall clock. It's almost one, and we're still at least an hour away from the city. 'Fifteen minutes is all we have.'

First, I Google her. A Tina Weikert comes up who paints dog portraits and sells them on eBay. But, a few more links lead me to her photograph, and I see that it's not our Tina Weikert at all.

Next, I try the online phone book. Mel checks out the Ridgewood High site to see if they have any alumni lists. We both hit dead ends.

'She's probably married,' Mel says.

I slap my forehead. Of course she's married! Who wouldn't be married with such a tiny nose!

We both sit silently for a moment, trying to figure out how you discover someone's married name.

'What a stupid thing to do! Change your name just

because you get married. I'll never change my name. Why should I? It's a holdover from an ancient male-dominated society. It has no place in tod—'

'Classmates.com!' I squeal, interrupting Mel's rant.

The librarian says, 'Shhh.'

'Don't they tell you how to reach old classmates?' I whisper to Amelia.

'Don't you have to pay them to do it?' she whispers back.

'Let's see.'

Fingers flying over the computer keys, I type in the web address for Classmates.com. Up pops a blank space that asks for my year of graduation, and a pull-down menu that requests the state my high school is in. I scroll down to New Jersey, and click on it. Next, I'm asked for the first letter of my high school. I click on 'R' for Ridgewood High. With each step forward, my hearts thumps harder in my chest. The next step is registration, but I notice, to my relief, that it's free. All I have to do is type in my name and email address.

T-I-N-A-W-E-I-K-E-R-T, I type.

'You don't know her email address,' Mel says.

I want to say 'Duh!' but she did come all the way out to New Jersey with me, so I restrain myself.

I type in the fake email address: *tinaweikert@i.love.randallsanders.com* and hold my breath. The last thing to do is to agree to their services (which, thankfully, doesn't require paying anything or signing over my soul) and click 'submit'.

I submit.

Mel and I watch the blue bar at the bottom of the page slowly fill in. We wait silently for the site to load. Then, there it is. A yellow banner reads: *View your class list.*

'Are we in?' Mel asks, leaning closer to the screen.

'I think we're in!' I say, blowing out a lungful of held-in air.

Almost too scared to scroll down, I clutch Mel's arm with my left hand and grip the mouse with my right. The names are listed alphabetically. It seems to take forever to reach the Ws. I go down and down until, all of a sudden, there she is.

Tina Weikert.

'Click on her!' Mel chirps.

I click. Instantly, Tina Weikert's profile page pops up. To email her, I must pay a membership fee. (I knew a fee would come in *somewhere*!). But, I don't need to email her. There, right in front of my face, is Tina Weikert's *married* name. Though she may have once wanted to be Tina *Sanders*, she's now Tina *Parker.*

Mel and I leap up and fling our arms around each other. Now, all we have to do is hope that Tina Weikert Parker never left Ridgewood, New Jersey.

THIRTY-THREE

Why isn't anything ever easy? I try searching for 'Parker, T Parker, Tina Parker, *Chris*tina Parker', every possible combination I can think of – but nothing comes up. My fifteen minutes of online time are almost over, and I'm getting nowhere fast.

'Maybe she's in the regular phone book,' Mel suggests.

Hey, why not?

While I keep looking online, Mel asks the librarian for a phone book.

'There's a *Ted* Parker listed,' she reports back to me, 'but no Tina.'

'Maybe he's her husband,' I say, hopeful, opening my handbag and pulling out my cell.

'No cell phones in the library,' the librarian calls from her desk. I sigh. Mel takes her trusty pad out and we jot down the number.

'Your fifteen minutes are up,' the librarian adds. Then, she walks over to us and asks, 'Find her?'

I answer what I desperately hope to be true. 'Not yet, but we will. Thank you for your help.'

*

On the front steps of the Ridgewood Public Library, I dial Ted Parker's phone number, hold my breath, and go boldly.

'Hello?'

'Is this Ted Parker?'

'No. He's my dad. He's at work.'

The voice sounds younger than me, but old enough to answer the next question.

'Is Tina Parker your mom?'

'Who wants to know?'

'I'm looking for Tina Parker, formerly Tina Weikert. I know this is weird, but is she your mom, by any chance?'

'No.'

My heart sinks. Mel sees me sag and drapes her arm around my shoulder.

'Okay,' I say, dejected. 'Thanks anyw—'

'She's my *aunt*,' the boy says.

'What?' Instantly, I perk up.

'Aunt Tina. She's married to my Uncle Brian. Or, *was*. They're divorced.'

'Are you sure?'

He doesn't say anything. Quickly, I add, 'I mean, that's great! Not about the divorce, of course.'

Mel gives me a weird look. Just to be absolutely sure, I ask the kid, 'Her last name used to be Weikert, right?'

'Who is this?'

Somehow, I don't think the pedicure line will work on a kid who probably *loves* his grubby fingernails.

'I'm calling from Ridgewood High,' I say. 'We're updating our records and contacting the class of ninety-four.'

With the ease of an Olympic diver, I dip back undercover. Mel shoots me a look, but thankfully doesn't say anything.

'Just a minute.'

The kid leaves the phone for a moment and my heart clutches. Is he getting his mom? Will she ask for ID? Did she *go* to Ridgewood High? Does she *work* in the administration office?

My panic escalates. Are they tracing my call? Are the police about to arrest me on the steps of Ridgewood Public Library? Do I watch too much crime TV?

'Hello?' He returns.

'Hi,' I say, trying to sound older and calmer.

'She lives in Connecticut. I can't find her number, but I have her email.'

'Email!' I squeal.

'If you need to call her, my mom has her number and she'll be home at about seven.'

'Email is perfect.'

He rattles off an email address, and I resist the urge to ask for his home address so I can mail him an invitation to the awards ceremony when I win a Peabody for inventive first-time reporting.

'Thanks,' I say, instead.

'Yeah,' he says, and hangs up.

Turning to Mel, I say, 'My days of being a nobody are numbered!'

My best friend hugs me and jokes, 'You'll always be a nobody to me.'

THIRTY-FOUR

You know how when one thing goes wrong, a *million* things go wrong right after it, like a domino effect? Well, amazingly, I discover that the opposite is also true. When something goes *right*, other things do, too.

'Bobbi Brown!'

As Mel and I run up Ridgewood Avenue, back to the train station, my eye catches a window display of Bobbi Brown cosmetics.

'Bobbi Brown will have the colour Nell's looking for,' I say to Mel, pulling her across the street.

A gorgeous make-up artist, dressed in black, looks like she could work for *Scene* magazine. When I show her my forensically-sealed pollen smear, and ask if she has an exact match, she looks bored and says, 'I don't think so.'

'It's for Nell Wickham,' I add.

'Nell Wickham? *The* Nell Wickham?'

'Yes. I'm her—' I almost say *servile toady*, but catch myself in time. 'I'm her assistant.' I flash my *Scene* ID.

'Why didn't you say so?'

The make-up artist scurries to the back room. 'Give

me one minute. I'm quite sure I can match this colour.'

'Exactly?'

'Of course.'

Mel and I try the make-up samples while we wait.

'Is it the real me?' Mel asks. Her lips are deep burgundy.

'Yes,' I say, 'if you're really Marilyn Manson.'

We giggle. Both of us are giddy with success. And, it's only one-thirty! If Bobbi Brown has a match, we'll even have time for lunch.

'Here you go.'

Holding a small pot of Bobbi Brown eye-shadow in one hand, and the pollen smear in the other, the make-up artist beams. Mel and I both gasp.

'It's *perfect*!' I say.

'We used this colour a lot last year.'

That, I decide, is something Nell doesn't need to know.

'How much?' I ask, hoping that Nell Wickham has an account here, too.

'Please tell Nell to enjoy it with our compliments,' she says, glowing.

I feel like asking, 'How much would it cost for someone who *didn't* make a gazillion dollars a year and couldn't afford to buy everything in this store?'

But, I don't.

And when the make-up artist hands me a small shopping bag filled with the latest Bobbi Brown products saying, 'Perhaps Nell would like to try some of these, too,' I resist the urge to snottily ask if Bobbi Brown tests on animals.

'If there's *ever* anything Nell needs – anything at *all* – please have her *call.*'

'I'll tell her,' I say.

On the way to the train station, I say to Amelia, 'How unfair is it that the richer you are, the more people give you stuff for free?'

Amelia, my wise best friend, says, 'It's not unfair, Susanna. It's *business.*'

THIRTY-FIVE

Okay, we did have lunch in Ridgewood. And I did insist on a small scoop of Chocolate Chip Cookie Dough ice-cream at Häagen Dazs. And we *did* miss the two-twenty train back to Penn Station. So, I shouldn't have been surprised when we got back to the city after four o'clock.

'Nell's going to kill me,' I screech, dragging Mel through the commuter mob in Penn Station. The two of us bounce against people like pinballs.

'Go!' Mel hugs me at the pathway to the cross-town shuttle. She's staying on the west side. 'Tell Nell you had a family emergency!'

A family emergency? To a woman who doesn't even consider a step-father, *family*?

'Thank you for today!' I shout as I race for the shuttle.

By the time I get to the lobby of the *Scene* building, I'm nearly hyperventilating. Mascara stings my eyes. Seventeen floors of air-conditioning don't come near cooling me off.

'Where have you *been*?'

Nell pronounces 'been' like 'bean'. One eyebrow is arched

so high it nearly flies off the top of her head. Her lips are so pinched together they look like a raisin.

'I was getting your pollen eye-shadow,' I stammer. Then I gulp. Loudly. Holding up the Bobbi Brown shopping bag, I say, 'They gave you extra stuff, too.'

Instantly, Nell's eyes light up. She reaches her hand out like a child and says, 'Gimme.'

Thankfully, the shadow *is* an exact match, and Nell forgets to interrogate me further the moment she pops open the clear top and smears it on her lids.

'It's fabulous, isn't it, Sue? Perfectly *mar*vellous!'

She looks like Big Bird.

'It's brilliant,' I say. Which is perfectly, marvellously true. If you use Webster's *first* definition of the word 'brilliant', which is, 'shining brightly'. Nell's eyelids could blind somebody if they caught sunlight at just the right angle.

'Well done, Susie,' she says, beaming.

'Thanks,' I say, turning to leave so I can plop into my chair, calm down, and email Tina Weikert Parker before Nell finds yet another way to butcher my name.

'Wait a minute, Suze.'

Crud. Too late.

'Where's my ripe mango?'

Oh *no.* In all the excitement, I forget to buy Nell's mango. Panic-stricken, I consider telling her there's a rare mango disease sweeping New York that mimics flesh-eating bacteria. But, that's a lie I could never pull off.

'I forgot,' I confess. 'I'll get it right now.'

As I turn to go, Nell says, 'Never mind about the mango, Susanna. I have an assignment for you.'

My heart stops. *Susanna? Assignment?* Is this instant karma for deciding against lying about the flesh-eating mango disease?

'I need you to get a story,' Nell says.

'A story?' My heart dances in my chest. Did she say what I *think* she said? A million things really *can* go right! Here I am, Susanna Barringer, standing before Big Bird Wickham, about to receive my first-ever reporting assignment for *Scene* magazine. Thank *God* I fessed up to forgetting the mango! This really *is* my lucky day.

'What's the story about?' I ask, barely able to keep from jumping up and down.

'Single celebrity moms,' Nell says.

I nod. It's been done before, but that's okay. I'll create a fresh new spin. Perhaps my angle will explore the *social* implications of celebrity single-parenthood. Is it okay for a movie star to have a child without being married, but not okay for a secretary in Boise, Idaho?

'Here.' Nell hands me a pad and pen.

I nearly burst into grateful tears. Taking the pad and pen, I wipe my sweaty forehead, sit and prepare to take notes on my first-ever big-time magazine assignment.

'Two Forty-Four East Sixty-Sixth Street,' Nell says.

Excitedly, I scribble the address. 'Who lives there?' I ask, unable to believe I'm about a meet a real CSM – celebrity single mom. Will it be Angelina Jolie? Jodie Foster? Diane Keaton?

'The writer, of course,' Nell says.

'Writer?' My brain scans every CSM writer I've heard of. Madonna wrote some children's books, didn't she? But, she's married now. It can't be her.

'The writer of the *story*, Susan. I need you to pick up the final page-proofs for her story on celebrity moms. She's going to a screening tonight and won't be able to get them in before her deadline. I told her not to worry. I have *you*.'

I swallow. The pen quivers in my hand.

'Excuse me?'

'She said she'd leave them with her doorman,' Nell says. 'Now scoot. I need to get that story in before I leave for the benefit.'

I can barely move, much less *scoot*. Somehow, I manage to stand and put one foot in front of the other until I'm out the door, in the elevator, through the revolving glass entrance, and back on the broiling streets of New York.

THIRTY-SIX

It's my turn to make dinner. Mom cooks on weekends while Dad is at work; Dad cooks Monday through Thursday; and I'm in charge of Friday night. Tonight, since the CSM writer's page-proofs were *not* with her doorman, and the subway took *for ever* to come, and the cross-town bus took even longer, I get home too late to make anything other than my last-minute speciality: Susanna's Freezer Stir-Fry. The secret is getting the wok *really* hot. Then, I pour in about a tablespoon of canola oil, two smashed garlic cloves to flavour the oil (remove in a minute or so), frozen veggies and microwaved chicken tenders. Season with soy sauce and a few drops of sesame oil and you're good to go. Dad likes rice with it, but Mom is off carbs and has convinced us to join her at dinner. Good thing, because real rice takes at least twenty minutes to cook and the instant stuff tastes like baby food.

'How was work today?' Mom asks, as she feeds The Trips a concoction of mashed bananas and pulverized oatmeal. In their highchairs, they look like three baby birds with their mouths hanging open and tufts of hair sticking straight up.

All I can do is grunt.

'You know,' Dad says, stabbing a partially-frozen broccoli floret with his fork, 'everybody has to pay their dues. You're not going to be editor-in-chief overnight.'

'I know,' I say. And I do. My expectations aren't *completely* out of whack. I realise a high-school kid won't be sent out to cover a movie premiere. I didn't think Randall Sanders would refuse to talk to anyone but me. Still, I *did* think I'd be doing more *assisting,* less fetching. I mean, I'd be happy to hold a microphone or tape recorder or help Keith Franklin tie his bandana. Anything in the action. Anything other than getting manuscripts and picking up fresh flowers (no lilacs!) and stroking Nell's precarious ego. Plus, I can't stand the thought of wasting an opportunity. If I don't make my mark now, I'll have to wait until after college! That's a *lifetime* away!

Dinner's ready, but I'm not hungry – the one good thing about feeling like a total loser.

'May I be excused?' I ask Mom and Dad.

Before either parent can answer, Henry flings a blob of mashed banana into Mom's hair, Evan starts to cry, Sam opens his tiny mouth even wider and bangs his palm on the highchair tray, and my parents have too much to do to even notice I'm alive.

Amelia has already IMd me.

Did TWP email u yet? she writes.

I respond with an instant message of my own: *NW put me back on slave duty. Emailing TWP ASAP.*

Then, my fingertips sit perched on the computer keyboard while I try to figure out what I'm going to say to the woman who holds my future in her hands.

Dear Mrs (Miss? Ms?) Parker (Weikert?): My name is Susanna (Barringer?). I understand you went to the prom with Randall (Randy?) Sanders.

Ugh. Already, it sounds like an email I would trash.

I start over.

Dear Ms Parker:

You don't know me. You have no reason to help me, but that's exactly what I'm asking you to do . . .

I bare my soul. I tell the truth. I even mention Nell's canary eye-shadow.

Here's my idea, I write. *I want to find out what Randall Sanders will say to his high-school prom date. I've seen him up close. I know he's a cool guy. I'm sure he'll want to talk to you and see what you've been up to.*

I tell her it's simple. All she has to do is call his agent and leave a message for him to call her back. When he does – and I'm sure he will – she'll tell me what they talk about. Nothing too personal. I won't invade her privacy.

I want to write an article about the real *Randall Sanders,* I type. *I want to find out something no one else knows. I want to show my boss what I can do. What do you say? Will you do it?*

Holding my breath, I hit the 'send' button.

Then I wait.

And *wait.*

THIRTY-SEVEN

It's Saturday. Mom ropes me into going to the Bronx Zoo. It's hot and crowded. The Trips are with us (of course) and they keep trying to wiggle out of their triple-decker stroller. When I tighten their seatbelts, they grab my hair with their sticky hands.

'Let *go,* Henry,' I say, annoyed. He does, just as Evan seizes another clump of hair and pulls.

'Pin your hair back in a ponytail, Susanna!' Mom says, testily.

Like it's *my* fault.

Nobody is in a good mood. Mom is tired, The Trips are cranky, and I haven't heard a word from Tina Weikert Parker in two weeks. More than thirty-three-and-a-third per cent of summer is over and I'm as close to being a celebrity-reporter as my brothers are to wiping their own muck off their faces.

'Do we really need to see wild horses?' I ask, copping a major attitude at the intersection between the Butterfly Zone and the elephants. 'Don't they look just like regular horses?'

'What do you want to see?' Mom asks.

'The parking lot.'

She gives me a look. 'I hear the gorilla exhibit is really special,' she says.

I roll my eyes. If you've seen one gorilla sitting in the dirt, you've seen them all. Still, I agree to make one last stop.

We follow the signs to the Congo Gorilla Forest, past the Mouse House, through the Dancing Crane Café. Mom buys two Dove bars. Ironically, The Trips munch on animal crackers. As we continue down the path toward the gorilla cages, I see a bunch of people in line.

'We have to *wait*? In the *sun*?'

'It'll move fast,' Mom says, handing me one of the Dove bars. 'Haven't you heard about this exhibit, Susanna? It's worth the wait.'

I sigh. Even though the zoo smells like a *zoo,* I must admit it's better than sitting home checking my email every five minutes. Peeling back the wrapping, I bite into the hard chocolate shell of the Dove bar for the first cool, sweet moment of the day.

Mom is right. The line moves fast. We're up at the ticket window just as I'm licking the last bit of vanilla ice-cream off my popsicle stick. The Trips have calmed down (maybe they're asleep!) and I'm feeling a happy little sugar rush. I take the stroller and push my brothers into another world.

Instantly, I'm blown away.

We're in a rain forest. It's warm and damp. Tree trunks rise up from the earth, vines twist in the air. Everything is lush and green. I hear a waterfall in the distance, and the *caw-caw* of tropical birds. Occasionally, I see one. But the leaves are thick and, like the real Congo, colourful flying shapes dart past your vision.

We continue down a path, walking deeper and deeper into the Congo. It smells good, like wet dirt. It's magical. The Trips are awake, and in a trance. I am, too. Now, I can't wait to see a gorilla!

Ahead, there's a building that's a dark, cool cave. We pass exotic monkeys hanging from tree limbs behind glass. The Trips squeal and clap their hands. I'm looking, but I don't see any big, hairy apes.

Until I turn a corner.

Mom and I both gasp. The Trips go silent. There, separated by only a thick pane of glass, is an entire gorilla family. *Inches* away. There are no cages. It seems like we're in a cage, if anything. The gorillas are free to roam in a huge habitat of green vegetation. A baby gorilla swings on a vine; another plays with its mother's human-like hands. And the father, a giant Silverback with a mondo-huge triangular head, sits by the glass and watches us enter his kingdom.

I'm mesmerised. I'm standing a foot away from a Silverback gorilla! He looks at me. His brown eyes take me in. I'm so close I can see his eyelashes. I feel as though I'm looking at a human. Maybe something even better than a human. I'm looking at a deep soul. It's undeniable.

'This is awesome,' Mom whispers.

I nod. I can't speak. As I stare into the gorilla's eyes, I'm certain he's telling me something. Inside my head, I hear the same four words over and over: *you can do it.*

My heart thrums. I can barely catch my breath.

Does this gorilla have some universal knowledge he's telepathically transferring to me?

You can do it.

'How?' I ask out loud.

Mom looks at me. 'How what?' she asks.

I don't respond. I just stare at the gorilla and wait for his silent answer. But the spell is broken. He's now playing with his big toe. Some pushy little kid shoves his way in front of me. The only sound I hear now is, 'Mommy, look at the monkey's funny black feet!'

It's okay. I can move on. The message has already been delivered.

You can do it.

Maybe the elephants can tell me how?

The second I get home, I can't wait to tell Mel all about the zoo and the gorilla's talkative eyes. Her cell is off, so I click my email on.

For the second time that day, I gasp out loud.

There it is.

Randall Sanders' prom date has emailed me back!

My right hand quivers as it hovers over the mouse. I'm afraid to click in. My whole life will change for the better or worse as soon as I read what Tina Weikert Parker has to say.

Finally, taking a deep breath, remembering the gorilla's message, I dive in. I open the email that will decide my future.

TWP has written two words: *Sorry, no.*

That's it. No explanation as to why she won't contact Randall Sanders. Just two words that instantly dash my hopes.

I'm devastated. My body melts into my desk chair and I sit there like a lump. Like a Silverback on a mound of green banana leaves.

Suddenly, I hear those four words in my head again: *you can do it.* I envisage Spence Silver's devastation when yet another batch of glue wouldn't stick. Did Little Frankie Epperson's popsicle freeze in an hour? I don't think so! I lift my head and hang my shoulders on a hanger.

Sorry to bother you again, I write TWP, *but would you mind telling me why not?*

I click 'send'.

Almost instantly, a reply comes back. This time, it's only one word.

Yes.

My heart sinks. Still, I don't give up.

This is my last question, I promise, I write. *If Randall Sanders called* you, *would you talk to him and then email me?*

Tina doesn't answer. I sit there for a full ten minutes. Nothing. Sighing, I get up and fall face-down on my bed.

From the living room, I hear my father tickling The Trips. Mom says, 'Bath time in ten minutes.' Then I hear one more sound. The *ding!* of new email.

In less than a second, I'm up and clicking my mouse. My hand doesn't quiver this time, but I do hold my breath.

There it is. An email from Tina. Again, it's just one word. One glorious word.

Okay.

And her phone number.

Like my little brothers, I clap my hands together and squeal. Operation Spence Silver isn't dead yet! All I have to do is get Randall Sanders – the hottest celeb in Hollywood – to pick up a phone and call the prom date he hasn't seen for over ten years. Then I have to get Tina Weikert Parker to call or email me to tell me what he says. How hard could it be? It's not like I'm inventing non-stick glue!

THIRTY-EIGHT

I think of nothing else all night. How can I get Randall Sanders to call a girl he hasn't seen since high school? Why should he help *me*, a nobody who was recently carted off his set? By the *cops.* Someone whose butt was internationally identified as belonging to a stalker?

Obviously, several ways to reach him are useless. Again, I make a list. Why waste time doing something that's doomed to fail?

DOOMED-TO-FAIL LIST

1. Showing up on the set again. Even if Randall Sanders is still shooting 'Caught Off-Guard' in Irving Place, the police will never let me past the barricades. And an arrest record really will kill my chances for getting into any good college.
2. Writing him a letter. He probably hasn't opened his daily mound of fan mail since his soap character, Brick Redman, married his stepsister after divorcing her mother.
3. Emailing his fan site. See above.
4. Renting a sky-writing plane. Too expensive. Plus, are sky-writing planes allowed in the airspace over Manhattan? Doubtful.

5. Sending him a lockbox from Chinatown. Been there, done that.
6. Calling him myself. Asking nicely. Believing in Santa Claus. Yeah, right.

Sitting at my desk, chewing on the back of my pen, ignoring the loud babbling of my brothers and insane *goo-gooing* of my mother in the family room, I focus my attention on what *will* work. At first, I can almost hear the tumbleweeds rolling through my empty brain. Then, I come up with an idea. It's so easy, I can't believe I didn't think of it before.

Grabbing a blank notepad on my desk, I scribble a note.

Call me when you have a moment.

Then I sign it, *Tina Weikert.*

My heart starts thumping. Immediately, I feel guilty. Is it forgery? Falsifying a document? Did I leave my fingerprints on the paper?

The answer to all three questions is 'yes'. Rats. Crumpling up the note, I toss it in the trash and resume chewing my pen. How hard can it be connecting two people who were once probably in love? Doesn't everyone want to find out what happened to their high-school sweetheart? If they *have* a high-school sweetheart, that is. Unlike me: Virginity Unlimited.

Dejected, I reach for the remote control of my TV. Perhaps another cable guru can enlighten me. As I flip the channels, and fall into the hypnosis of flashing images and sounds, the answer suddenly smacks me in the face.

'Of course!' I say out loud.

In the next second, I'm back at my desk, back at my notepad, writing another note. This time, I don't forge anyone's name or care if my fingerprints are on the page. I keep it real, just as Menu Man instructed me to do.

R:

Call Tina Weikert at (917) 555-6306.

SB

It's not lying. My initials are SB after all. It's simple, real and – I think with my heart doing flip-flops – it just might work.

Folding the note in half, I tuck it into an envelope and address it to Randall Sanders in care of the *Caught Off-Guard* show. Monday morning, on my way to fetch Nell's flowers, I'll do what I've done all summer: be a messenger! Wearing dark glasses and a baseball cap, I'll hand-deliver the note to the guard at the set's barricade. It's just a note. At least he'll give it to Randall Sanders' assistant. And, at the very least, she'll ask her boss if he knows a woman named Tina Weikert. His eyes will light up. He'll grin, get one of those faraway looks and mutter, 'I wonder what ever happened to her?'

His assistant will grin, too, and say, 'Why don't you call her and find out?'

He will. (Who wouldn't?) And my career as a celebrity-reporter will begin!

THIRTY-NINE

Monday Morning 9:46: The deed is done. The note has been passed over the barricade. No one recognised me as the 'Stalker Butt'. The wait begins.

At work, Nell has restarted Phase One of the South Beach diet and I am on my way to find organic chicken sausages.

Monday Afternoon 2:16: My email inbox is full of spam. Nell takes her shoes off and asks me if I think she needs bunion surgery. I say, 'No way,' then I look up bunions in the dictionary and think, 'Well, yes.'

Monday Late-Afternoon 4:52: Mel reminds me to meet her in the hospital cafeteria for our weekly, after-work lemonades. I tell her I can't because I'm expecting an email from TWP.

Monday Night 11:47: No word yet. Were Post-It Notes invented in a day?

Tuesday Morning 9:38: Nell has a haircut appointment this morning, so I am free to stare at my inbox until message from TWP comes through.

Tuesday Afternoon 4:15: Dad emails to ask me why my cell is turned off. I confess I'm hiding from Nell, who just got a hideous haircut and is making everyone pay. Dad replies by asking me to pick up Pampers on my way home from work.

Tuesday Night 11:52: Wondering about little Frankie Epperson and his popsicle invention. Did it freeze right away? Or did it take its own sweet time?

Wednesday Morning 8:32: Florist tells me he offered to deliver Nell's daily flowers himself, but she refused. 'Susan lives to serve me,' he said she said. I swear, that's what he said she said!

Wednesday Afternoon 2:35: Nell decides she hates meat, South Beach, and the entire state of Florida.

I check my email. Zippo.

Wednesday Night 12:05: Come to think of it, Columbus sailed for *months.*

Thursday Morning 8:37: Outside, a bee lands on the flowers I pick up for Nell. It burrows deep in the petals. I trap it in the cellophane wrapping and hear its angry buzzing. Nell sure will be surprised when she unwraps her flowers!

No email yet.

Thursday Afternoon 4:17: I call Amelia and ask if I can visit Edgar. I need a laugh. Decide to pick up a jumbo chocolate chip cookie on the way.

Thursday Evening 5:46: Edgar's face is grey. Mel and I both have a sinking feeling. But Eddie insists he's not ready to start 'Phase Two of his cosmic adventure'. Phase *Three,* he says, involves visiting a new solar system. At least that's what he hopes.

Thursday Night 1:08: Can't sleep. Can't believe RS hasn't called TWP. Or did he call and she hasn't emailed me yet? Did he call and she'll never email me? Check email once more before IMing Amelia and asking her if she's awake, too.

Friday Morning 9:47: Snippy email from Mel telling me the IM *ding* woke her up last night. What, she doesn't know how to turn her computer off when she goes to bed?

Friday Afternoon 3:36: Nell asks me to take the elevator down seventeen floors so I can tell her driver that she's going to be five minutes late to go to the Hamptons. It's the *second* time she's asked me to do that. This time, the driver says,

'Why don't you just call me instead of coming out here?' He gives me his cell number and I return to my desk so I can cut out an old magazine photo of Nell and stick a pin in it.

No email yet.

Friday Night 6:38: Order take-out Chinese food instead of cooking dinner. Need extra time to stare at my empty email inbox and mentally *will* an email from TWP.

Saturday Morning 10:30: Ask Mom if I can call a computer repair-man. She emails me from her computer and concludes nothing is wrong with my system. She's right. It's my *life* that's falling apart.

Saturday Afternoon 2:17: Take The Trips to Hudson Park again. With all their crying, they don't notice that I'm wailing too.

Saturday Night 1:48: That *New York Times* article was right. Sleep deprivation really *is* a problem among today's teens.

Sunday Morning 10:10: Pray. I'm a bit rusty, but I hear it's like riding a bike.

Sunday Afternoon 1:29: Nell calls me *at home.* She left her favourite Jimmy Choo sandals on the bathroom floor of her apartment. Will I get her key from her doorman, find the shoes, and drive them two hours to the Hamptons so she can wear them tonight at a benefit for something *else* that's endangered? I'm speechless. As soon as my jaw starts working, I remind her I'm too young to drive. 'Oh,' she says. Then she hangs up.

Sunday Night 7:15: My pillow smells like my shampoo. I wonder how long I can bury my face it in without suffocating. I decide to find out. Amazingly, it turns out to be hours, though I finally fall asleep before I pass out. At least I think I do.

Week Two: I hate Christopher Columbus, Spence Silver, little Frankie Epperson, Nell, Tina Weikert Parker and, yes, even Randall Sanders. I was *totally* wrong about him. He probably bought his mother a house as a tax *deduction.*

FORTY

Sixty-six-point-six per cent of my summer is over. The daily editorial meeting is in progress. Nell sits on her white throne, a skimmed-milk mozzarella stick between her fingers like a cigar. Keith Franklin leans back against the white cushions of her couch. He looks even hotter without his bandana. His black hair is perfectly curly – not too wavy, not too kinky. Dishevelled enough to look as though he just rolled out of bed. Sasha, the fashion editor, wears a long, narrow, halter dress. Black, of course. Her milk-chocolate skin is so smooth and perfect, I want to touch her arm to see if she has make-up on it. Renée, the senior editor and Nicole Kidman look-alike, chats with a new editorial assistant, Bennett, who looks like Will Smith.

Me? I'm wearing beige Capri pants, a turquoise-blue T-shirt, and Keds. My hair is held up with a claw clip.

Yes, I've given up.

I know, I'm a native New Yorker. But, there's only so much I can take before even *my* DNA is damaged.

'Susan, will you get coffee and tea for us?' Nell asks, as the meeting begins.

'Sure,' I say. Why not? What else have I got to do? Nell's fresh flowers are on her desk, her cheese stick is dangling out her mouth, her Manny Blah-Blahs are on her bunioned feet, and nothing needs to be messengered . . . yet.

'The usual?' I ask.

The roomful of gorgeous heads nods. As I leave Nell's office for Starbucks, I glance out the window. The sun is bright, a woman sits at a computer screen in the office building across the street, horns honk below, and somewhere – out there – Tina Weikert Parker is living her life without even thinking of me once.

Amelia was no help.

'What did you *expect*?' she'd asked, when I'd mentioned that weeks had passed without a word.

If I'd told her the truth, I would have said, 'I expected Randall Sanders to call TWP instantly, and then she'd email me with intimate details of their conversation. After that, I'd write an article for *Scene* magazine titled "I Knew He'd Call", and Nell's eyes would bug out of her recently *thermaged* face when she realised her little messenger girl was a born reporter. She'd beg me to drop out of school and work for *Scene* full-time, but I'd refuse and promise only to return each summer – and *maybe* at spring break.'

Instead, I lied and told Mel I didn't really think TWP would email me, but I'd *hoped* she would. Then I added, truthfully, 'I guess I really am just Nell's toady.'

*

As I pass around the coffees, and set a plate of carbed, uncarbed, proteined, fruited and vegan edibles on the centre table, I hear Sasha say, 'I'd like to do a piece about stars replacing models on the runway. It seems to be a trend.'

'Brilliant,' Nell says. 'What else?'

'One of my sources tells me to watch Jessica Alba. She's taking off,' says Renée.

'Fabulous,' coos Nell. 'Do we have enough photos of her, Keith?'

'I'll get more,' Keith says.

'Lovely!'

It's Friday. I can't wait for the weekend so I can sleep for forty-eight lovely hours straight.

Renée asks, 'Anybody know what's ahead on HBO?'

Nell's phone rings. Carmen picks it up. I place a few napkins on the table.

'Susanna?'

To make the spread more stylish, I fan the napkins out.

'Su*sanna.*' Carmen holds the phone in the air. 'The phone is for you.'

My head jerks up. 'For me?' I ask, stunned. The only calls I ever get are from Amelia, on my cell.

'Put it on speaker,' Nell says, annoyed.

'That's oka—'

My call goes on speaker. With everyone listening, I silently pray it's not my father asking me to buy Pampers on my way home for work.

'Susanna Barringer?'

'Yes.'

'This is Tina. Tina Parker.'

My eyes pop out of my head. Nell, still irritated by the interruption, asks, 'It this an *emergency*, Sue?'

I swallow. 'I'm in a meeting right now, Ms Parker. Can I call you back in fifteen minutes?'

'Sure,' Tina says, 'I'm just calling to invite you to be my guest at the premiere of Randall Sanders' new movie tonight.'

FORTY-ONE

I now know how it feels to be in the middle of one of those crazy Midwestern storms. Tornado Nell pelts me with a million questions.

'What the . . . ?! How did you . . . !? Who is Tina Parker? Do you *know* Randall Sanders? What else are you keeping from me? Pick up the phone, Susanna!'

I pick up the phone. 'Tina?'

'Can you talk now?' she asks. I tell her I can, but honestly, I'm having trouble getting actual words out of my mouth. Not only is my heart thumping in my ears, but my throat is constricted in shock and I can barely breathe because Nell, Keith, Sasha, Renée and Bennett are crowded around the telephone, trying to hear what Tina Weikert Parker has to say. The conversation goes like this:

Tina: 'Can you make it?'

Me: 'Uhhhuhhh.'

Nell: 'Of course she can!'

Tina: 'I'm inviting you, Susanna. Only *you.* No one else from the magazine.'

Me: 'Oh. Uh.'

Renée: 'What did we do to *her*?'

Bennett: 'Who is this Tina person, anyway?'

Tina: 'You'll need a fancy dress. Do you have one?'

Me: 'Nuhuhh.'

Sasha: 'Don't worry. I'll find *something* that fits her.'

Nell: 'Will *anything* fit her?'

Tina: 'Do you know where the Ziegfeld Theatre is?'

Me: 'Nuhuhh.'

Keith: 'Fifty-Fourth, between Sixth and Seventh.'

Tina: 'You know what? Randy is sending a limo for me. I'll pick you up when I get into the city.'

Nell: 'Randy? How perfectly brilliant!'

Me: 'Limo?'

Bennett: 'Who *is* this woman? Keith, do you know who she is?'

Tina: 'Where do you live?'

Keith: 'What's her name again?'

Me: 'Uh, lower west side, meat-packing district.'

Renée: 'I just looked at a condo there over the weekend! It's fabulous, if you can stomach the smell.'

Nell: 'You're moving, Renée? I know someone's who's looking.'

Sasha: 'Tina something, I think. Maybe Gina?'

Tina: 'Do you want me to call your parents?'

Renée: 'I'm not moving. I just like to snoop.'

Me: 'My parents?'

Tina: 'For permission. There's a big party afterwards.'

Nell, Keith, Sasha, Renée and Bennett: 'The after-party!'

Me: 'Uhhh.'

A premiere party? With *Randall Sanders*? I nearly pass out. Thankfully, the staff are squishing me so tightly I'd never fall to the floor.

Renée: 'I practically offered to sleep with the publicist to get invited to that party! It didn't work.'

Bennett: 'He's gay.'

Me: 'Yeah, calling my parents would be good.'

I manage to give Tina Weikert Parker my phone number and address. She tells me she'll call my parents, then – if it's okay with them – she'll pick me up at seven.

Nell: 'It'll be *fine* with her parents. If there's any problem, have them call me.'

Tina: 'Susanna?'

Me: 'Yes?'

Tina: 'Thank you.'

Sasha: 'Shhh! I didn't hear what she said.'

Keith: 'She said, "Thank you".'

Bennett: 'For what?'

Me: 'For what?'

Tina: 'A lot.'

Sasha: 'For *what*?'

Renée: 'She said, "A lot".'

Tina: 'We'll talk more when I see you, okay?'

Nell, Keith, Sasha, Renée, and Bennett: 'Okay!'

Tina hangs up, I hang up, and the *Scene* magazine tornado spins me off to prepare for the most exciting night of my life.

FORTY-TWO

Nell's manicurist arrives first. She takes one look at my fingernails and says, 'Good Lord.' By the time she's moved down to my feet, she's shaking her head and repeating, over and over, 'Thank God I got here in time.'

Bennett has his hands in my hair.

'Does it always just *lay* there?' he asks.

'No,' I answer. 'It usually does sit-ups.'

He disappears for a moment, returning with hot rollers that he plugs into an outlet in Nell's office.

Sasha, still on the phone, shouts, 'If you can't get me a size twelve by four o'clock, I'm pulling you out of the next issue.'

'I'm an eight sometimes,' I say weakly. 'Or a ten.'

No one responds.

Nell has spent the past hour in the art department redoing the magazine's layout to accommodate the story I'm going to tell when I return from tonight's premiere and (*gasp!*) after-party. Keith already gave me a tiny digital camera with instructions to 'point and shoot at everything'. His dream celebrity photo? 'An A-list actress eating bread, a star dancing like a spaz, a married celeb making out with someone other than their spouse, or *anything* from inside the men's or women's restroom.'

'The men's room?' I ask.

Bennett answers, 'If your hair doesn't fluff up, sweetie, no one will question it.'

I feel like Cinderella getting ready for the ball. It's surreal. I, Susanna Barringer, am now the story. When Nell asked how on Earth I was able to snag an invite to the hottest ticket in town, plus the *impossible*-to-get-into private after-party, I began with the train ride to New Jersey.

'*New Jersey?*' she'd said, as if I told her I'd been to Mars and back.

As I explained how I found 'Randy's' yearbook and Tina's email, I could see my image change before their eyes. I, Susanna Barringer, servile summer toady, became a *reporter.*

'Francesca?' Nell says, while the whole staff is crowded around me, 'We're going to be here a while. Fetch more bottled water, will you?'

I glance at her, she sneers at me.

Nell says, 'Unless you'd like something else, Susanna. Are you feeling peckish?'

FORTY-THREE

I *am* Cinderella. My coach – the limousine – waits in front of my apartment building. I'm wearing a gorgeous brown satin Jeffrey Chow dress, spiked Jimmy Choo shoes, a Miu Miu evening bag and dangling Juicy Couture vintage earrings. Names I just memorised today.

'Trust me,' Sasha said. 'You're well-dressed.'

I have no idea how much it all costs, and I don't want to know. Tomorrow, I turn back into a pumpkin. Tonight, I'm going to meet my Prince Charming wearing the coolest clothes ever. And they *fit* perfectly!

Since Dad is at work, Mom emails him a photo of me in my premiere outfit. He IMs one word back: *Wow*. Which is just how I feel. *Wow*. My hair isn't flat, and the satin dress looks like ripples of chocolate kissing my knees. Though it took about half an hour of practice to walk normally on my sparkly gold Jimmy Choos, I'm now confident enough to make my way down a red carpet, and into my destiny.

'You look beautiful, honey.' With Evan strapped to her back, Henry on one hip, and Sam on the other, Mom kisses my cheek and asks, 'You ready for the paparazzi?'

We all crowd into the elevator and descend five flights. A limo with smoked windows idles at the curb out front. Mom and The Trips waddle over to the passenger door and open it.

'You must be Tina Parker,' Mom says, peering in.

Tina steps out of the limo saying, 'My goodness. You have your hands full!'

I recognise her immediately. She still has long blonde hair, though it's lighter and more frizzy than in her high-school photo. Her tan looks bottled, and her arms, bared in a sequinned white halter dress, are over-muscled. Something about Tina Parker's face looks sad – her eyes are a fake contact-lens green, and her lips are dark orange. My first impression is that she tries too hard. Mom always says, 'Better to show your age naturally, then unnaturally cover it up and look like a circus clown.'

Which is why the sum total of my hippie mom's make-up is a tube of Aveda tinted moisturiser, the soft red lipgloss she loaned me for tonight, and Maybelline Great Lash mascara that's still in the package.

Tina *doesn't* look like a clown, but she *might* in a couple of years.

'I'm Susanna,' I say, holding out my hand.

Tina Parker hugs me and says, 'I'm so glad to meet you.'

We climb into the limo and I sink into the cool black leather seat.

'Take good care of my girl,' Mom says, shutting the door.

The limo smells like Tina Parker's vanilla perfume. The driver – actually wearing a chauffeur's hat! – is seated so far up, we have to shout to talk to him. As we pull away from the curb, I wave to my mom and my brothers, but I don't think they see me through the darkened windows.

'We're off!' Tina says.

My heart pounding, I actually pinch my arm to make sure I'm really here. No way is this happening to me! I, Susanna Barringer, am in a limousine on my way to the premiere of Randall Sanders' first major movie, *The Man in the Window.* And the after-party! The tiny digital camera is in my 'Meow Meow' bag, and Nell's instructions are in my head. *Get a great story, Susanna. We're counting on you.*

I smile. Ever since TWP called in the middle of the editorial meeting, Nell Wickham hasn't forgotten my name once.

The ride uptown to the Ziegfeld Theatre is magical. Suddenly, I'm a person behind smoked windows! At a stop light, two girls peer through the glass. Tina and I just laugh.

'Boy would they be disappointed if we rolled down the window,' Tina says.

'Let's not,' I reply, giggling.

We ride in silence, staring at the flickering city lights as they flash by the window. Abruptly, Tina Weikert Parker turns to me and asks, 'Are you wondering why I invited you tonight?'

Well, *yeah,* if 'wondering' is a synonym for 'going insane with curiosity'.

'I have been a little curious,' I say.

Tina takes a deep breath. She runs a squared-off fingernail under one eye as if a tear is about to escape. I try to sit up, but the soft leather seat has swallowed me.

'Your little trick that got Randy to call me actually forced me to face some of my demons,' she begins.

'Uh huh.'

'Without going into detail, my life has gone downhill since high school. Believe it or not, those were the best years of my life.'

High school? The *best* years of her life? Man, her life really has taken a nosedive.

'I'm sorry,' I say.

'Don't be,' she says back. 'I made my own bed.'

We snake through traffic on Fourteenth Street, turn left on Fifth. Then, almost accidentally, Tina Weikert Parker opens her mouth and spills every detail of the past fifteen years.

'Randy and I had everything in high school,' she begins. 'We were both popular and athletic. And Randy – well, he was special even then. You couldn't help but love him. And he loved *me.* I couldn't believe it. We were inseparable. We lost our virginity to each other.'

I nod. Try to look like I, too, lost my virginity to Randy.

'You know how the intensity of a high-school romance can take over your life?' Tina asks.

'Not really,' I answer, honestly. If she knows I'm a virgin, will she stop spilling her guts? 'But I can imagine it,' I add, quickly.

'Randy and I were together at school, after school, on the phone at night, on weekends. It freaked me out.'

'Freaked you out? Who would be freaked out being with Randall Sanders twenty-four seven?'

'Me,' Tina says, smiling sadly. 'I was pulled-together on the outside, but an insecure mess on the inside. After a gazillion years of therapy, I now know that I didn't feel I deserved a guy like Randy, so I did a lot to screw things up.'

I stifle the urge to nod knowingly. I've always suspected that those popular, thin, blonde, perfect girls in school were nut jobs inside! I just knew it! Besides, who's good enough for Randall Sanders?

Tina inhales. The memories are so fresh for her, I can see the pain on her face.

'I slept with Randy's older brother,' Tina blurts out.

My Juicy Couture earrings hit my cheeks as my head turns.

'I hurt him badly. It was the dumbest thing I've ever done. In one stupid night, I killed our chances for a future together.'

Tina cheated on America's Hunk?! I'm speechless.

'I probably shouldn't be telling you any of this,' Tina continues, 'but I heard that Randy was so upset he almost took a dive off the George Washington Bridge. I doubt it's true, but that's what people were saying.'

Oh *God.*

'My life has been a series of failures. I dropped out of college, hopped from one bad relationship to the next, married a loser, drank too much. See this scar?'

Tina points to a Harry Potterish lightning bolt on her chin.

'I cracked my chin on the steering wheel when I hit a railing on the Merritt Parkway. I'd been drinking since lunch.'

Tina wipes under her eye again.

I want to ask her, 'Can one guy really send you on a death spiral?' But, I know the answer. Of course. If that guy is Randall Sanders.

'If it wasn't for the programme, I'd be dead,' Tina says.

All of a sudden, I wonder why TWP is telling me this. My initial nosiness has turned into squirmy discomfort. Maybe I *don't* having the makings of a celebrity-reporter after all. This is all *too* real. I feel like a kid in a grown-up dress and overpriced shoes overhearing an adult confession. Which is exactly who I am and what I've done. My impulse to cover my ears is almost as strong as the desire to hear more.

As the limousine turns right on Fifty-Fourth, and crosses Seventh, I see beams of light crisscrossing in the air. A surge of excitement mixes in with the rest of my emotions. Now, I'm not sure at all that I'll be able to gracefully walk the red carpet.

Tina sniffs and says, 'I was too ashamed to face Randy again, after all these years. He's done so well, and I've screwed up my life.'

A row of limos slows traffic. I can't help stealing a glance out the window even as Tina bares her soul. I mean, I'm almost at my first-ever private screening! I'm wearing a Chow and a Choo!

'Because of you, Susanna,' Tina continues, oblivious to the excitement ahead of us, 'Randy called and we talked and he forgave me. I hadn't spoken to him in years. Because of you, I can make amends for my mistakes and let go of the past. I can forgive myself for the terrible thing I did.'

'I'm glad,' I say, truthfully. Tina squeezes my hand. The limo stops. 'But, I really need to brush my hair now.'

At long last, TWP looks out the window and sees what we're about to walk into.

'My goodness!' she says, 'How do I look?'

My summer with Nell has taught me well.

'You look fabulous,' I say, 'better than Halle Berry.'

Tina beams. She pulls a mirror out of her purse and reapplies her Day-Glo lipstick. I glide Mom's gloss across my lips, fluff up my curls. I hear shrieks through the window. I see fans straining at a velvet rope – the rope that I'll soon be on the *inside* of. My lips are stuck in a wide smile.

'This is going to be the coolest night of *both* our lives,' I say.

'Are you ready?' Tina asks.

'I'm ready.'

At that moment, the driver opens the limo door, and I step out into my destiny.

FORTY-FOUR

It passes in slo-mo. A white-gloved hand reaches for the door handle on the limo. It opens. A swell of cheers and girly screams rise into the air. My heart beats so fast, I nearly take flight. One foot pokes out the door, then another. I rise up, step out. I wobble. But, I quickly regain my footing.

Paparazzi and press, with their gargantuan camera lenses, are huddled behind the rope. Bright lights blind me. There are so many camera clicks it sounds like a Flamenco dancer. It's impossible to find Keith Franklin in the crowd of photographers, though I know he's there. I can feel him smiling for me.

As suddenly as it started, the camera clicks stop. The lenses point to the next limo. The screams die down as soon as the crowd sees that Tina and I are no one. But, I *feel* like someone. I can't stop grinning. The (red!) carpet squishes beneath my feet as I glide toward the theatre door. My satin dress swirls around my knees.

'Susanna!'

I turn. It's Keith. He's made his way to the front of the line, away from the other photographers. His signature bandana on his glorious head, Keith flags me over. No way can I wrap my mind around the fact that Keith is on the outside of the velvet rope and I'm on the *in*!

'Let me take a picture of you both,' Keith says.

Standing with Tina's arm around my waist, I can barely breathe, my heart is thudding so hard. Other photographers hustle over to shoot us, too. If Keith Franklin is getting a shot, we must be *someone.*

'Now let me get one of you alone, Susanna,' Keith says.

'Me?'

'For my wallet,' Keith says, grinning.

I beam. I pose in my amazing dress and feel like a movie star.

Someone shouts, 'Who are you wearing?' Thrilled, I turn to search for Joan and Melissa. Only, it's some girl with straggly hair and a worn autograph book. And, she's asking *Tina*, not me.

'Loehmann's back room,' Tina answers, giggling. 'Half-off.'

If Tina only knew how much money I was wearing!

Keith lets his camera hang on its strap, and he reaches one hand up to my head. Before I have enough time to freak out, he cups my neck, pulls me toward him, and kisses my cheek.

'Don't forget, you're *working* tonight,' he whispers in my ear. 'Keep your eyes and ears open.'

*

At the glass entrance to the theatre, a huge man in a suit asks for our invitation. Tina pulls it out of her handbag and the man takes it, nods, then unhooks the final velvet rope and lets us in.

In. Here I am, Susanna Barringer, chronic striver, on the *inside* of the most-talked about movie premiere of the year. My head is spinning. I want to turn around and go back to the beginning of the red-carpet walk. I want to feel my Jeffrey Chow brush against my knees as I wave to the fans. I want to sign an autograph book.

'God, I wish I still drank,' Tina says, nervously.

Alcohol? No way would I want to be even slightly impaired during the most memorable night of my life.

'I only drink sodas now; shall I get us two?' Tina asks.

'Yes, please. Anything diet.'

The lobby of the Ziegfeld Theatre is plush and packed with people. It smells of custom perfume, professional hair styling, fresh manis and pedis, expensive eye cream and cologne that *isn't* Old Spice. The women wear dresses like mine, that probably cost as much as my parents' rent. The men wear suits with hundred-dollar T-shirts underneath.

'Here.' Tina hands me a Diet Coke. Her hands are shaking. She takes a deep breath and says, 'Ready to find Randy?'

The mere mention of his name sends my heart on another beating spree. I follow Tina through the crowded lobby and repeat three words over and over in my head: *Do Not Scream.*

Demi is there, and Ashton, as is Whoopi, Scarlett, Mary-Kate, Ashley, Justin, and (I nearly faint) the *real* George Clooney. He's so hot, I can't stop staring.

'Is that . . . ?' Tina whispers.

'Yes!'

They all look so . . . so . . . nearly *real*! Except, of course, the models.

Tyra is chatting up some short, bald guy. Gisele is beside them, sipping champagne. As I had with Keith's model-friend, Monique, I can't help but notice what freaks of nature they are. No one in real life could be that tall, that thin, that cheekboned and that perfectly cleavaged. Whose thighs don't touch *at all*, even when their ankles are pressed together?

Toward the back of the room, a crowd of people is huddled around someone. My heart is now pounding so hard, I'm sure my chest is bruised. Tina tiptoes up to the crowd, and then I hear it. *His* voice.

'Tina!'

Like an oyster reluctantly opening its shell, the crowd parts and Randall Sanders – my pearl – steps out.

'I'm so glad you could make it,' he says to Tina, hugging her tightly.

Standing behind them, inches from Randall Sanders' beautiful face, I lock gazes with the man of my dreams. I'm frozen. Like the Silverback's eyes, Randall Sanders' eyes are brown and deep and full of soulful thoughts. My heart aches to think he was once in such despair he wanted to end it all. How could Tina cheat on a such a loving spirit?

Looking in those eyes, I'm now sure he bought his mother a house – not as a tax deduction! – but because she is the woman who worked two jobs so he could go to Yale Drama School. It was out of love, and respect, for *all* women. Looking into Randall Sanders' eyes, I see that he is definitely worthy of my endless devotion. He is kind and sensitive and loving—

'Hey, aren't you the girl who was stalking me?'

FORTY-FIVE

I'm going to kill Keith Franklin! I'm going to yank that stupid bandana off his head and choke him with it. It if wasn't for Keith's photo of my big fat butt being put on a bus beneath *Scene* magazine's big fat lying headline, Randall Sanders never would have labelled the girl in the Choo and Chow a 'stalker'. If it wasn't for Keith Stupid Franklin, I wouldn't be standing here right now, beet-faced, sweating into a gazillion-dollar dress I have to return to the fashion closet, unable to string two words together, in front of my all-time favourite actor, and a whole wad of important people waiting for me to be carted off (again!) by the cops.

'She's with me, Randy,' Tina, my saviour, says. 'She's the girl I told you about. Susanna.'

'Oh, yes,' Randall says. Then he looks at me and laughs. 'You're a reporter?'

I swallow. Suddenly, I remember Nell's instructions. *Get a great story, Susanna.*

'Yes,' I say, my voice as squeaky as one of my brother's squeals. 'I'm a reporter for *Scene* magazine.' I don't even believe myself.

In a moment I will lock in a mental time capsule for the rest of my life, Randall Sanders unfolds himself from Tina Parker, steps in front of me, takes my hand, kisses it, and says, 'Make sure you only report nice things.'

All I'm able to do, because I'm an *idiot*, is giggle and nod.

Then, Randall Sanders pulls me close and kisses my cheek exactly where Keith Franklin had.

'I'm trusting you,' he whispers.

For the rest of my life I'll feel the soft, warm puff of Randall Sanders' trust against my ear.

FORTY-SIX

Now I truly know what they mean by *buzz.* The stellar crowd buzzes in the theatre lobby, they buzz as they find their seats and settle in for the movie, and after the final credits roll and the roaring applause dies down, the buzz swells again for the rest of the night. Plus, there's the buzzing in my heart. I am the luckiest girl in the world.

'Fabulous!'

'His best work yet!'

'I smell a Golden Globe!'

Compliments dart through the air as Tina and I make our way out of the theatre. I can't speak. The images of Randall Sanders are still swimming through my brain. To see his beautiful face movie-screen large is almost too much to bear.

In the theatre lobby, the same suited giant who took our invitation at the door shouts, 'Please take the private bus out front to the party. Your limos will be waiting for you at the restaurant.'

Private bus! Limos waiting! I've spent my whole summer standing at stinky bus-stops or steamy subway platforms.

Now, a beautiful, smoke-windowed, celebrity-packed *private* bus is waiting at the curb for me!

A mob of fans is still crowded outside. One yells, 'How was the flick?'

Still unable to speak, I flash an enthusiastic thumbs-up.

He asks, 'Are you anybody?'

I laugh. Yesterday, the answer would have been a quick 'no'. Today, I feel differently. My neck is longer and my hands swing more gracefully. In a moment of reckless abandon, I turn to the guy and wink. Let *him* figure out who I am.

Tina and I climb aboard the bus and choose two upholstered seats toward the front. The air-conditioning is blasting. It's chilly inside, but who cares? Sean Combs just passed by me. The hem of his cream-coloured jacket brushes against my arm.

'Was that . . . ?'

I nod. In silence, we watch famous people board the bus. I try not to stare, but who can *not* stare when Spiderman walks by?

'Randy said he'll meet us there,' Tina says.

'Is it . . . ? Is he . . . ?' I struggle for the right words.

'Yeah,' she says. 'It's okay.'

The bus engine revs up and the celebrity caravan pulls away from the curb.

Five blocks later, the bus pulls in front of another red carpet and stops. We probably could have walked faster (definitely, if I was in my Keds instead of my Choos), but it's so much more fun to sit high above the pedestrians and watch them wonder who's behind those dark windows. At the entrance to Cipriani, closed for this private party, the bus door opens and spits us all out. Again, Tina is asked to present her invitation. Again, I feel like a movie star. I can't believe I'm about to walk into a party that Renée couldn't even *sleep* her way into!

The after-party is like a mini-premiere. There's a red carpet and a velvet rope. And I'm on the *inside* of it. Camera-flashes light up the sidewalk as we make our way to the entrance. Keith Franklin yells, 'Who's the babe in the Jeffrey Chow?' I spot him in the crowd and wave.

A cool blast of air hits my face as I enter the private party. The room is *gorgeous.* The ceiling is so high, you can barely see the detailed wood-carving and gold trim. It feels like a church, but Tina tells me it used to be one of those fancy old banks. Flowers are everywhere. Round tables, with white tablecloths and glistening crystal glasses, dot the room. Buzz still fills the air. Bright teeth light up the shadows. Manicured hands – both male and female – hold thin glasses of golden bubbly. People air-kiss each other. Music is coming from somewhere, but the room is so large and packed with people I can't see a band.

Inside. As I stand there, taking it all in, I think about that word: *inside*. Now, I know how it feels to be let in instead of left out. It feels like floating. You feel *weightless.*

'My two biggest fans!'

Feeling my Jeffrey Chow brush my knees, I wheel around and there he is. 'Besides my mother, of course,' Randall says.

I can't move. I can only stare. He's glowing.

'You were amazing,' Tina says, kissing Randy's cheek.

I nod so hard I can hear my neck crack. One of Randall's eyebrows is sticking up – the one near his scar. And I see a few grey hairs at his temple. Which makes me love him even more. He's so . . . so . . . *human.* A tuft of blond chest-hair pokes through the open collar of his white shirt. It looks so soft, I can barely keep my hand from touching it. He smells like wet dirt and apricots. His teeth are perfect piano keys. And hi—

'Hey! Where's your chip?' I blurt out.

Randall Sanders runs his tongue over his front tooth. 'Porcelain veneer,' he says. 'Thank you for noticing.'

Tina says, 'We both loved the movie, Ra—'

'Oh my God. You were *awesome*!' I squeal. 'The movie was incredible. I loved it. I can't believe I'm here.'

Suddenly, my voice appears.

'That scene where you slide down the fire escape, was that really you?'

'All me,' Randall Sanders says. 'It took four days to shoot and I had blisters on my blisters.'

I laugh hysterically. 'It reminded me of the scene in *The Clock Ticks Backward* when you slid down the staircase.

Or the time when you were on that roller-coaster in *Caught Off-Guard*!'

Randall grins. 'You really *are* my biggest fan.'

'I am!'

As if overtaken by an alien, I babble uncontrollably about every show he's ever done. I ask him if it was hard playing a serial strangler; if he'll ever do a soap again. I tell him about Edgar and the hospital and – to my horror – how we're both glad he shaved his moustache. Tina stands there watching my lips flap.

'My best friend Amelia thinks I'm crazy to love you. Well, not "love" in the stalker sense. More like "love" in the, you know, *admire* sense.'

'Hungry, Susanna?' Tina asks me, finally, when I take a breath.

'No way! I ate tons of popcorn during the movie, but I almost choked on it when that guy popped out of the dumpster and started chasing Randall with a knife!'

Tina and Randall share a look. I know I should stop chattering, but my nerves have taken over my mouth. Thankfully, Tina saves me by saying, 'I'm starving. Let's get something to eat, okay? We'll catch up with Randy later.'

'That would be great. It was really, really nice to talk with you Mr Sand—'

Before I can finish, Tina steers me away from Randall Sanders, and we get in the buffet line.

'That wasn't me,' I say, mortified. 'It was my insane twin.'

'Randy has that effect on young girls.'

I bury my face in my hands. 'He thinks I'm a blathering idiot, doesn't he?'

'He probably thinks you are who you are – a kid.'

How can I argue with the truth, especially on the greatest night of my life?

FORTY-SEVEN

As it had on the red carpet, the evening seems to pass in slo-mo. 'Randy' makes his way around the room, shaking hands and kissing cheeks. Other stars are there, too – Hilary Duff, Usher, Orlando Bloom, Kirsten Dunst, Nicole Richie. It's obvious why they are called 'stars'. They're lit from within.

As Tina and I stand in the buffet line (behind Beyoncé!), I try to memorise every moment so I'll remember it for life. Then, I hear Keith's voice in my head. *Don't forget, you're* working *tonight.*

'The movie was awesome, don't you think?'

Beyoncé turns around. She wear a sparkly gold mini-dress, and gold shoes that are so high, I can't see how anyone could walk on them. But *she* can. As the buffet line moves, so does Beyoncé. And no one can take their eyes off her.

'Yes,' she says to me. 'It was cool.'

I'm staring at the most beautiful woman I've ever seen. Her skin is polished copper, her hair is a tumble of soft blonde curls, and her eyes belong to a panther.

'Were you *ever* ugly?' I blurt out.

Beyoncé laughs.

'I mean, when you were a teen. Did you have zits and bad hair days and crushes on boys who thought you were a loser?'

'Susanna!' Tina steps up and grabs my arm.

'It's okay,' Beyoncé says. 'The truth is, I *still* have those days.'

It's impossible to believe it, when I watch her move around the buffet table like a Greek goddess. Still, it was nice of her to say. Quietly removing my camera from my 'Meow Meow' handbag, I snap a quick shot of Beyoncé picking up a piece of French bread.

The moment I smell hot food, I'm starved. Circling the buffet table, I see pasta with red sauce, chicken with white sauce, and grilled vegetables with black char lines. I choose a little bit of everything – I want to taste it all.

'My shoes are killing me,' Tina says, making a beeline for the nearest empty table. Her plate is filled with grilled veggies.

Astoundingly, my feet feel fine. Maybe these shoes *are* worth four hundred dollars.

Tina doesn't say much while she eats. Which is surprising, considering she told me *everything* in the car. I think she's as overwhelmed by the event as I am.

'Are you okay?' I finally ask.

She take a deep breath. 'I'm a little sad, that's all.'

Sad? Who could be sad when Derek Jeter just walked by and – I *swear* – he smiled right at us!

Tina softly says, 'I look around and see what my life could have been. If I hadn't been such a jerk.'

Eventually, Tina Parker and I get up and wander around the party.

'Will you be okay on your own while I find the restroom?' she asks me.

'Okay?' I say. 'I'll be in heaven!'

Tina leaves and I'm left to do what I love to do most: observe celebs in the wild.

Instantly, I discover the biggest advantage to being a nobody – no one sees me. As I weave around tables and waiters and women who wear diamonds the size of headlights, no one pays any attention. They don't even notice me when I point my camera and click, or hover about, sipping diet cola and overhearing conversations.

'She's the next Julia.'

'He's the next Leo.'

'There's no stopping Randy,' someone else says. 'He's the next Depp.'

Tidbits of gossip float into my ears as I stroll around the room.

'Is Orlando still seeing Kate? He's here alone.'

'Kirsten Dunst is *tiny.* She reads much bigger on screen.'

'Who is Nicole Richie, again? Why is she famous?'

'I hear Randall Sanders is gay. He must be. He's here alone.'

I almost bust into the conversation to inform the gossipers that Randy is here with *me.* And, of course, his high-school sweetheart. But, I know better than to violate the first rule in celebrity-reporting: *never stop the gossips. They keep us in business.*

So, with camera in hand, I continue drifting around the room with my eyes and ears open.

'That Usher can usher me anywhere he wants!'

By the end of the most awesome night of my life, I've come to realise one truth about celebrities: if you subtract their impossible thinness, the gleaming white teeth, the muscular shoulders, the haircuts and highlight jobs that cost as much as my Choos, the designer bling, the smooth, hairless skin, the pouffy lips, and the supernatural glow that bathes them in celestial golden light, they're *nothing* like you and me. True stars are *born*, not made.

FORTY-EIGHT

'Susanna!'

My heart lurches. Nell got my name right. Her voice is singsongy. Does this mean she's read the article I wrote over the weekend and loves it? Could this be the beginning of the brand new me?

'Su*sanna*?'

No one yells bad news down a hall at work, do they?

'Yoo-hoo! Are you out there?'

I stand, my legs wobbly, and make my way to Nell Wickham's open office door.

'There you are!' she says. 'The woman of the hour!'

Woman? Hour? I beam.

'Sit, please, darling.'

Please? Darling? I sit. Boldly, I cross my legs.

'Tell me about the premiere,' Nell says. 'I want *all* the dirt!'

'Well,' I begin, 'it was *awesome.* Randall Sanders sent a limo all the way to Connecticut to pick Tina up, and she picked me up. Walking down the red carpet was unbelievable. I saw Keith there, when I wasn't blinded by camera-flashes in my eyes! And, I didn't trip, which I was totally afraid I'd do.'

Nell nods and smiles encouragingly.

'Inside the theatre, it was *gorgeous.* Stars were everywhere.'

'Such as?'

'You name it, practically!'

Nell, still smiling, asks, 'Was alcohol served?'

'Yes. But I didn't have any.'

'Of course not. Did any of the celebrities, say, have too much to drink?'

'No. Not that I know of.'

'Did Tina drink?'

'No.'

'Okay. Go on.'

'The movie was *awesome.* It's definitely going to be a huge hit. And, afterwards, there was a private bus out front waiting to take all of us to the party. It was so cool. A bus just for us!'

Nell's broad smile begins to look odd. Like it's pasted on her face.

I focus on the tip of her nose, and continue.

'There was a live band at the party, but no one danced much. Mostly people just stood around the room and drank champagne. Oh, and Kirsten Dunst asked me for the time.'

Her weird smile is beginning to freak me out.

'I didn't spill anything on the dress,' I say.

Now she's not blinking.

'Uh, Nell,' I venture, 'did you happen to see the article I left on your desk?'

Still grinning maniacally, Nell says, 'Yes! It was *adorable*! What a clever girl you are!'

Adorable? Clever? Girl? I have no idea if that's good news or bad.

Gathering courage, I ask, 'So, do you think you might want to publish it in the magazine.'

Nell doesn't hesitate. There's no moment of suspense. She simply throws her head back and howls.

'Publish it? In *Scene*? How perfectly ridiculous!'

Ridiculous. Now, that's a word that leaves no room for interpretation.

Still laughing, Nell says, 'This is a national magazine, Susan, not the high-school paper! Your article was a Hostess Twinkie. We don't publish fluff!'

I'm back to being 'Susan'. My chin quivers. I feel tears gathering in my eyes. My summer of slavery and arse-kissing – not to mention my train trip to Jersey, schemes, plans, dreams – are all dashed in one hideous blow. I'm crushed.

Magnifying my humiliation, Nell reads the entire article, out loud, from marshmallow-filled beginning to end.

'Prom Date Reunion, by Susanna Barringer,' she begins, her British accent a piece of glass in my ear. 'What would you say if your prom date called today? Especially if you're one of the hottest stars in Hollywood. Would you talk to him or her? If so, what would you say? That is the question one of *Scene* magazine's roving reporters asked America's Hunk, Randall Sanders. His answer is the stuff of every prom-goer's dream.

'*Randy* Sanders graduated Ridgewood High School in New Jersey over ten years ago. His high-school sweetheart, Tina Weikert, knew he was special, even then. But, nobody knew he'd become the Randall Sanders that would first steal our hearts as the wicked Brick Redman, then wow the world with his acting talents on the small screen and large. How does stratospheric success change someone? That's what this reporter wanted to find out. The answer: if you're Randall Sanders, you're always going to keep it real.

'Far from forgetting those he left behind, Randy invited Tina (now Tina Parker) to the premiere of his blockbuster new movie, *The Man in the Window.* He introduced her to other superstars, models, directors, even the catering staff as, "my first love". Tina couldn't stop smiling. Who could?

'Once again (as if we need more proof!), it's easy to see why America is in love with its national hunk. He's as nice as he is nice-looking. Exactly what this up-and-coming celebrity-reporter suspected all along.'

The silence in Nell's office swallows me up. I'd hide under her desk, but it's *glass.* She looks at me as if I'm a toddler with chocolate pudding on my face. Or, more accurately, a silly teenager with the sticky filling of a Hostess Twinkie smeared across her beet-red cheeks.

'Susan.'

My shoulders have slipped so far off their hanger, they're in a heap on the floor. I don't answer, afraid my voice will crack.

'Haven't you learned anything all summer?' Nell asks.

I'm tempted to burst into tears and list every subway and bus route, how to refill toner in the copier, and my personal technique for carrying fifteen different beverages without spilling a drop.

'What do you mean?' I ask, instead, biting my inner lip.

Nell puts my article down and says, 'Magazine publishing is a cut-throat business. You can't make a go of it unless you give the readers what they want – *dirt.* You've given them suds.'

My parents were right – this is a slimy career. Maybe I *am* damaging my corpus callosum!

'Besides, you're a *kid,*' Nell continues. 'You should be hanging out in malls and making-out with pimply boys. Not writing magazine articles.'

When's the last time Nell saw a hang-out mall in Manhattan? And, I want to tell her, she doesn't have to rub it in that I can't even get a *pimply* boy to make-out with me.

'What's your rush, Susie?'

Now, it's 'Susie'. In five more minutes, it's going to be, 'Sue, will you scratch my back? A little lower. Ah!'

'*Star Trek,*' I say.

Nell blinks.

'I want to boldly go where no girl has gone before.'

Nell blinks again.

'This summer was my shot to show you what I can do,' I say.

'Ah.' Nell's voice softens as she says, 'You've been very helpful to me, Susan. Just watching you all summer has given me scads of ideas for *Teen Scene.*'

Like what? I want to ask. How to dress for stress?

'And now you can help me even more,' she says.

Getting up from behind her desk, Nell circles around and sits in the chair next to mine. Her eyes are two black lasers.

'You had a lengthy limo ride to the premiere, right?' she asks.

'It wasn't *that* long.'

'Long enough to get to know Ms Parker a little?'

'A little.'

'Did she tell you anything *interesting* about our Randy boy?'

'Interesting?' I swallow.

Nell leans forward. 'Not sudsy.'

'Well . . .' I remember about Tina and Randy losing their virginity together, about her sleeping with his brother, about his rumoured plan to take a header off the GWB. I feel the imprint of Keith's whisper in my ear: *keep your eyes and ears open.* Nell told me to get a great story. I'm the girl who said she'd do *anything.* Even hide in poopy garbage!

All of a sudden, I feel like the naïve, stupid, kid that I am. My 'job' that night was not to write a puff piece on my favourite actor, but to dig up dirt from his high-school sweetheart!

Nell says, 'Just paint me the broad strokes. Renée can fill in the details.'

Man! How could I be so dumb?

Tina knew I was a wannabe reporter, still, I'm sure she never imagined that the stuff she told me in the limo would end up in the next issue of *Scene* magazine. I could see the headline now: America's Hunk Contemplates Suicide When High-School Sweetheart Shags His Brother.

'Susanna.' Nell's voice was gentle. 'If you ever want to make a living as a celebrity-reporter, you have to ferret out information they don't want you to know. That's how you get an exclusive. That's how the game is played.'

I nodded. I knew that much from my day with Keith Franklin. *Squeeze information out of them so gently they don't feel the pinch.*

'You're serious about one day having a career, aren't you?' Nell asked.

'Yes.' My voice is weak.

'Then tell me what Miss Tina had to say.'

I try to swallow, but my tongue is sandpaper. I feel Randall Sanders' breath on my cheek. *I'm trusting you.*

'She told me they were inseparable. Twenty-four seven.'

Eyebrows cocked, Nell asks, 'And?'

'And then they broke up.'

'That's it?'

I shrug.

'Why did they break up?' Nell asked. 'Another woman? Another *man*?'

Is this what it takes to make it? Do I have to give the readers what they want, no matter whom I hurt or betray? Tina should have known better, right? I *did* tell her I wanted to be a reporter, didn't I? Who did she think she was talking to? A *kid*?

I look directly at Nell – my soft, gooey insides a mess.

'I haven't the faintest idea.'

FORTY-NINE

She'll be surprised. So will he. But, that's not why I'm on the subway to the hospital. I'm rumbling underground because I want Edgar to put my failure in perspective. I want Mel to drape her arm around my shoulder and tell me it was right to take the high road even if it makes you feel low. I want them both to make me laugh and remind me I have years to figure out what *else* I want to do with my life.

The nurses' station is deserted when I get off the hospital elevator. I hear the monotone of television news. Someone coughs. Suddenly, I'm scared. What if today is Edgar's day to sign out? Is that where everybody is?

As I had done before, I creep down the dim hallway toward his room. My heart pounds. Please God, I whisper under my breath, not today. Please, not today.

Edgar's door is open halfway. I hear someone talking. The voice is familiar, but it's not Mel and it's not Edgar. My pulse hammering, I take a step toward the door, push it open and can't believe my eyes.

'Randy!' I shriek.

Edgar's room is packed. Nurses line the back wall, other

pink-smocked volunteers crowd around the window, Mel is stationed at Edgar's feet, and Randall Sanders stands at the edge of his bed.

'Can you believe it?' Mel shouts across the room, her face flushed.

'No,' I say, too stunned to say anything else.

Edgar beams. Randall says to me, 'This is the guy you were talking about, right? The one who hated my moustache?'

Now I'm too floored to formulate *any* words. I simply nod and let my jaw hang open.

'We're shooting on the west side today, so I thought I'd drop in for a few minutes,' Randall says, 'Eddie is a real trip.'

'He gave me a DVD of *The Man in the Window*,' Edgar says, 'so I can watch it here.'

'Remember – no bootlegging, Eddie. That DVD is from my private stash.'

Edgar puts his hand over his heart. 'I swear on my life,' he says, with a maniacal grin.

The scene is surreal. I can't believe Randall Sanders was even listening when I nervously chattered about his movies and Edgar and the hospital. And now he's *here*? He actually walked through the front door and talked to the admitting nurse and took the elevator up to the Palliative Care Unit and found Edgar's room? How awesome is that?

I notice that Edgar doesn't reach for his morphine button at all. And, as I glance around the room, I see angelic smiles on everyone's faces. Even several doctors who are standing there, grinning. All because of Randall Sanders. Just by *being* there, he's made everyone's day. Maybe even their month or year. That's the true power of celebrity, I think. And, with Edgar, Randall Sanders' visit is much more. It's a painkiller – a human drug that makes even *dying* easier to bear.

I sigh.

Why can't *this* be the story everyone wants to read?

FIFTY

Summer is almost over and Plan B is a total washout. Here I am, standing on the subway platform, sweating, waiting for the express train to Wall Street. Nell instructed her accountant to refuse a messenger service because she has me – a girl who once lost a shoe on an airplane! – to 'fetch' her documents and bring them back to her.

It's cool. Even though I'm about to faint from the heat, I've come to embrace the realities of my summer job. I'm a servile toady. That's what I do.

Since the premiere and after-party – and seeing Randall Sanders in Edgar's room – I've been thinking about my future. And my here and now. I cancelled my membership in the *Access Hollywood* online community. With Mel's help, I've even formulated a new career strategy. I call it Plan C.

PLAN C

1. Stop being obsessed with celebs; start caring about real people.
2. Ace high school.

3. Consider boosting de-virginising odds by boldly going into a male-dominated profession (my idea).
4. Consider joining the Peace Corps (Amelia's idea).
5. Reconsider Marine Biology. Maybe become a dolphin trainer at a water park? At least it will be cool in summer. They don't have to wear bathing suits, do they??
6. Think deep thoughts. Worry about low-income housing instead of J Lo's multiple spousing.
7. Thank Nell for her part in making me a better person. My life in the shallow lane is officially over.

Back at the office, I push through the revolving door into the marble lobby. Flashing my *Scene* magazine badge, the guard waves me through the metal detector. The air-conditioning feels yummy as I stand at the elevators clutching Nell's personally-retrieved documents in my sweaty hands.

It's late afternoon. I press the seventeenth-floor button and feel the elevator slowly rise. One more week, I say to myself. After that, the *profound* me will emerge.

'Hi, *Ah*-strid,' I say to the receptionist.

She raises one eyebrow, buzzes me in. I practise empathy by putting myself in her pointy shoes. Instantly, I'm cranky and starving.

'Have a nice day,' I say. I know it's lame. But, in this heartless world, couldn't we all use a little smiley face?

'Get me the Gwen and Gavin file!'

'What?! You *promised*!'

'She's our next cover! Who left that honking zit on her face?'

The black bees are running down the halls, screaming into their cells and shouting over the partitions. It's business as usual.

In her office, Nell is flipping through a stack of glossy photographs.

'Susie-Q!' she says, as I walk in and hand her the papers from her accountant. Then she leans back in her chair and says, 'Tell me honestly, do I need a breast reduction? My implants are a D.'

With a thoughtful expression, I examine my boss' boobs.

'They're *you*,' I answer honestly. 'Excellent cleavage.'

Nell bites her lip, looks as though she might cry. 'That's what I'd hoped,' she says, 'but you never can be too sure.'

'Do you need anything else?' I ask. 'Organic green tea? Turkey jerky?'

'No. I'm detoxing for two weeks. Nothing but cranberry juice and water.'

'Ah.' I smile. 'I'll be at my table. If you need me, just yell.'

Since I've decided to deepen my shallow self, a sense of calm has engulfed me. So what if I spent the summer being a slave! I'm a better person now. How many people can say *that* after spending the summer fetching?

'Keith is looking for you,' Carmen says as I pass her desk.

'Thank you.' I smile angelically, my shoulders on a very enlightened hanger.

Keith is at the light board in his office, his back to the door. I take in the V-shape of his torso, the way his black curls hug his neck, the muscles bulging out of both arms. Even in the super-cool air-conditioning, he's totally hot.

'You wanted to see me?' I say.

Keith turns around. 'Susanna. Come in and sit down.'

As ever, his front is as gorgeous as his back. I forgave him for putting my 'stalker butt' in the magazine and causing Randall Sanders to recognise me at the premiere. How could anyone stay mad at a guy with three dimples? (Two cheek, one chin.)

'I read your prom date piece,' Keith says.

I groan. 'Nell is circulating it around the office? Is everyone getting a good laugh?'

'I thought it was good.'

'Yeah, right.'

Keith smiles. 'It was young, inexperienced, cute, and earnest. Just like you.'

Cute? Did Keith Franklin just call me cute? I sit up. It's my virginal curse to instantly quiver whenever a hot guy even slightly veers close to attraction. Then I stop. Maybe he said 'quiet'. Did he say 'cut'? No, that's definitely not it. No way would Keith, or anyone else, ever describe me as 'cut'. But, I *was* pretty quiet on our day together. Mostly, I was listening to him. Would that classify me as 'quiet', or just a good listener? Clearly, I'm not a good listener if I didn't even hear him call me 'cute'. Or, was it 'quiet'?

'Susanna?'

'Yes.' I smile, try to look cute. I don't say anything else in case he really meant 'quiet'.

'We may even end up using some of the photos you took at the party.'

I beam.

'Your work is green, but I think you definitely have a future in magazines.'

'You do?'

'I do. So does Nell.'

'She *does*?'

'She says you have pluck.'

'Pluck? Like removing chicken feathers? Which is probably what she'll ask me to do next.'

Keith laughs. I feel a squirt of adrenaline shoot through my veins. My sweaty palms leave an imprint on my khaki Capris. Virginal curse, continued.

'We need an assistant to help us out in March.'

'March? I'll be in school.'

'It'll only be for a long weekend. Nell will talk to your parents.'

A *weekend*? In spite of my new enlightened self, I feel anger constricting my throat.

'Nell can't detox herself or fetch her barfy eye-shadow or stroke her own royal ego for one lousy weekend? Her shoe budget alone could support a small nation! Can't she pony up the dough for a *butler* instead of me? No way! Forget it!

I'm *busy.* Besides, I'm refocusing my career goals – the Peace Corps or Habitat for Humanity or maybe the water girl for an international men's soccer team.'

Keith laughs so hard I can almost see his vocal cords.

'Actually, Susanna,' he says, 'I need you to help *me.*'

I swallow. 'You?'

'*Mostly* me, I should say. It's a crazy weekend, so we need someone who can help out all over, if necessary.'

'I don't get it. What's so special about March?'

'Oscar.'

'Oscar who?'

'It's not Oscar *who,* it's Oscar Night.'

I freeze. Did I just hear what I just heard?

'We'd fly you out to Los Angeles, put you up in your own hotel room. You'd probably miss a day of school. Nell will talk to your par—'

'Did you say *Oscar,* as in Academy Awards' Oscar?'

'The naked gold guy himself.'

My heart pumps so hard I can feel it in my skull.

'Nell, Renée, Sasha, and I will be going this year. If your parents say yes, and you want to go, we'd like to tak—'

I shriek. The same uncontrollable noise that shot out of my throat when I first saw Randall Sanders, and again when I saw him in Edgar's hospital room. Leaping up from my chair, I dash for Keith and fling my arms around his gorgeous neck.

'The Academy Awards?' I yelp. 'The *real* red carpet?

Hollywood? Julia? Jack? Jude? You want me to go with you?'

All thoughts of deepening my character disappear. The Academy Awards isn't shallow! It's . . . it's . . . the Academy *Awards*!

'Yes, Susanna, if you don't choke me, I want you to go. I'll even pay you as a freelancer. Not much, but more than you're making now.'

I try, but I can't let go. A freelancer! How will I *live* until March?

'Why me?' I ask, finally loosening my grip on Keith's neck.

Keith faces me squarely. 'Anyone who can hook a celebrity up with his prom date can do *anything*. Even Nell thinks so.'

I *love* Nell. Her boobs are stellar! No wonder she's the editor-in-chief. She's *brilliant*!

'You'll be working primarily with me,' Keith says, 'which mostly means carrying my stuff and spotting stars who are trying to hide. You up for it?'

Am I up for it? Has Joan Rivers run out of facial skin to lift? Does Star Jones sound like Darth Vader? Will Katie Holmes secretly take Prozac to handle living with her whack-job hubby?

'I don't know what to say,' I sputter, nearly weeping with joy.

'You've earned it, Susanna. If you decide against the Peace Corps, or that water gig, you're going to make a great reporter one day.'

'I am?' I sniff.

'You are. Now get back to work. God knows what Nell's detox will bubble up. You may need to book an exorcism.'

Skipping out of Keith's office, I sing, 'See you in March!'

My head held high, I pass senior editors in their corner offices, associate editors in their cubicles along the window, assistant editors in their cubbies, and fact-checkers and editorial assistants at their desks along the wall. One day, I'll have a *desk*, I say to myself.

I, Susanna Barringer – the luckiest girl in the world – will be the celebrity-reporter who makes a difference. The reporter who *celebrates* celebrity instead of exploits it. Yes! That's what I'm destined to do. That's my passion!

Thank you, universe.

Move over Joan and Melissa!

Hollywood, here I come.